Duty to Mitigate

Based on a true story

Balbinder Chagger

Duty to Mitigate

Based on a true story

This first edition published in 2021 by Balbinder Chagger

Copyright © Balbinder Chagger 2021

All rights reserved

The moral right of the author has been asserted

The right of Balbinder Chagger to be identified as author of this work has been asserted in accordance with the Copyright, Designs and Patents Act 1988

Without limiting the rights under copyright reserved above, no part of this publication may be reprinted or reproduced or utilised in any form or by any electronic, mechanical or other means, now or hereafter invented, including photocopying and recording, or in any information storage or retrieval system, without the permission in writing from the author.

Cover photograph, design, typesetting, and art by Balbinder Chagger

www.dutytomitigate.co.uk
balbinder.chagger@dutytomitigate.co.uk

ISBN 979-8-595-97679-4

For

Sumitran and Harbhajan

ABOUT THE AUTHOR

Duty to Mitigate, a work of fiction based on a true story concerning unfair treatment at work, is Balbinder Chagger's third book. It is the sequel to *Burden of Proof*, his second book. Balbinder has many years of employment history across several international investment banks. His first book, *Options Explained Simply: The Fundamental Principles Course*, is a work of nonfiction based on his financial knowledge.

CONTENTS

1	Unlawful Basis	1
2	Provisional Intention	10
3	Long Way Short	26
4	Incomplete Process	47
5	Ranjit Singh's Update Testimony	72
6	Sarah Rigsby's Testimony	127
7	Angela Paxton's Testimony	135
8	Respondents' Case	144
9	Claimant's Case	155
10	Judgement Day	167

1

UNLAWFUL BASIS

~ Friday 15th December 2006, 12:30 p.m. ~

'Mr Singh, do you choose reinstatement or compensation?' the chairman asks addressing me directly from his seat at the judges' bench high up on the raised platform at the head of the courtroom. He sits in the centre seat, the back of which protrudes twelve inches above the seats of the two judges flanking him.

'Hmm,' I contemplate sitting in the public gallery immediately behind my counsel and her assistant, on the far right hand side of the courtroom, feeling relieved and immensely grateful that the tribunal upheld every single one of my claims against Neil and the bank.

Neil, having just listened to the tribunal rule that he discriminated against me racially in dismissing me from my job, sits calmly maintaining a poker face. He awaits my answer, as do Simon, Veronica, and the bank's other officers sitting with him in the public gallery immediately behind their counsel, on the far left hand side of the courtroom. Their counsel, sitting at her desk with her assistant beside her, stands by for my reply. The members of the public, sitting behind us in the gallery, anticipate my response. The two judges flanking the chairman look down at me, waiting.

'Er,' I stall.

'Mr Singh,' the chairman says looking up at the clock on the wall to his right, 'your answer may wait until after lunch, over which time you may choose to take counsel'. Addressing the two counsels, he says, 'it is now twelve-thirty. All parties are to reconvene for one-thirty. The hearing is adjourned'.

'All stand,' the courtroom attendant cries out.

We all rise to our feet. The three judges rise from their seats, turn to their right, file towards the door to their chamber in the wall behind the judges' bench, and disappear through it. The people in the public gallery begin to make their way along the aisles towards the door at the back of the room to exit. My counsel, her assistant, and I join in the flow. Outside the courtroom, we make our way along the corridors to the claimants' waiting room, and go in. There are three other parties in there already, counsels and claimants with friends and family members. We take up the free seats around a low, circular-shaped coffee table in a corner at the far end of the room, with the full-length window looking out on to Kingsway.

'Congratulations on winning your case outright, on every single point,' my counsel says with a sense of heartfelt joy in her face, 'and with a unanimous tribunal!'

'Congratulations to you too,' I reply smiling triumphantly. 'And, thank you! It wouldn't have been possible without you, and also without my solicitor's good work. He'll be waiting on tenterhooks. We'd better phone him and tell him the great news'.

'I've already texted him,' she says. 'He's over the moon, and very relieved. He sends his congratulations. Celebrations will have to wait, I'm afraid. We need to get ourselves ready for the next hearing session. We don't have much time'.

'Yes,' I reply. 'So,' I say getting down to business, 'reinstatement means the bank re-employs me back in my Market Risk Controller role it dismissed me from, as though the dismissal never happened?'

'Yes,' she replies, 'if that's possible. If not, then it means re-employing you in another role, on terms and conditions as close as possible to your original role's'.

'I see,' I reply. 'Does it also mean I'll get paid all of the back pay I've missed out on since I was dismissed?'

'Yes, it'll make good all of your back pay,' she confirms.

'That sounds great,' I say.

'Reinstatement,' she continues, 'is the *primary* remedy in law for a wrongful dismissal. It has the status of primary remedy because it restores the *full* value a dismissal deprives a claimant of. Compensation can't do that. Hence, compensation is the *secondary* legal remedy'.

'What do you mean?' I ask.

'Compensation can only restore the *economic* and *financial* values your dismissal deprives you of,' she says, 'like, your salary, bonuses, healthcare, and any other benefits that can be monetised. It can't restore the *non-economic* kinds of values you got out of your employment, the emotional and the psychological values, like, the enjoyment of performing the job, social status, self-esteem, and so on. Those things don't have a monetary value. Compensation can't cover them. Reinstatement restores all those kinds of things as well as the economic values. Reinstatement is the superior remedy, in that respect'.

'I see,' I reply.

'Although reinstatement is the primary remedy for an unfair dismissal,' she continues, 'a tribunal can't consider it unless the claimant authorises it to do so. A claimant might not want to be reinstated after all that's happened. Most claimants don't. So, the tribunal needs the claimant's explicit consent to be able to consider reinstatement. That's why the chairman started the remedy hearing by asking you whether you want to be reinstated or not?'

'Okay, I understand,' I reply.

'If you choose reinstatement,' she continues, 'then that doesn't automatically entitle you to be reinstated. Your choice merely authorises the tribunal to be able to consider reinstatement as a *possible* remedy. It has absolute power and discretion, though, as to whether to grant or refuse you your choice'.

'How does it decide?' I ask.

'Based on whether reinstatement can actually work in the circumstances,' she says. 'It'll look at things like, whether your motives for wanting reinstatement are sincere, and whether workable relationships remain after all that's happened. It'll investigate whether you're in any way, even partly, to blame for your dismissal. If it finds you are, then it'd hardly be right to reinstate you'.

'True,' I reply. 'But, I'm not to blame'.

'It'll also consider the respondents' points of view,' she continues. 'They might not want to reinstate you. Then, it'll need to give them the chance to put their case and to show good cause for not wanting you back'.

'Okay,' I say. 'The other option is to forget reinstatement altogether and go straight to compensation'.

'Yes,' she says, 'and that's what I recommend. Employers hardly ever want back employees who litigated against them, and tribunals hardly ever award reinstatement. The nature of employment disputes and litigation is vexatious. It tends to ruin completely the relationships between the parties. It renders the relationships unworkable. There's usually residual hurt and bitterness lingering on both sides, meaning reinstatement won't actually work in practice. In my entire twenty-year career so far, I've never managed to convince a tribunal to award reinstatement to any of my clients'.

'I see,' I reply. 'That all sounds reasonable enough'.

'Besides,' she continues, 'even if a tribunal orders reinstatement, the order is unenforceable. The bank doesn't have to comply with it because there's a higher rule in this country that says parties can't be forced together if any one of them doesn't wish it. My advice is, save yourself the time and the considerable costs of a hearing on reinstatement. Go straight to compensation'.

'If I do get reinstated,' I say, 'then I'll be back in my job. I'll be employed again. I'll be paid my back pay, and my future will be before me as though I were never dismissed. I won't suffer any damages, except all the money I've spent so far on seeking justice'.

'Correct,' she says. 'In employment tribunal cases, tribunals can't order the loser to pay the winner's costs. All the costs you incur in seeking justice are yours to bear, I'm sorry to say'.

'Right,' I reply.

'Even though they've been found guilty of every single complaint against them,' she says, 'neither Neil nor the bank have even apologised. The last thing they'll tolerate is having you back. They'll object to reinstatement, for sure. Then, the tribunal will conclude the relationships aren't workable, because that's easy and usual for tribunals to conclude. It won't award you reinstatement. Then, the remedy will have to proceed to compensation. You may as well move to compensation right now and save yourself the time and the significant costs of a detour through reinstatement'.

'Reinstatement's an opportunity to bring things to an amicable end, right here, right now,' I say. 'There's great value in that. There'll be no need to have a risky, and probably lengthy, hearing on compensation. Reinstatement will end litigation immediately. There'll be no risk of appeals. No need to incur any more legal fees. I've been unemployed for eight months now. I have no money coming in at all, and I'm gushing money on legal fees. My savings are running out fast. I can't afford to keep litigating for much longer. I'm worried. Neil and the bank have nothing to lose by reinstatement, and much to gain. As their employee again, I'll be under a duty not to speak out against them. They'll have power and control over me again. If they want, they could exploit the position to better engineer my dismissal at some future date, or drive me into an untenable situation where I just decide I have no choice but to resign and leave. The benefits to them are great. They're a corporation. To them, I'm just a cost figure in a spreadsheet that they need to manage and contain. They've already spent a fortune on me, just to end up achieving a massive, public fiasco. Reinstatement's a safe and cheap option for them. It's an opportunity for them to take complete control of the situation and manage it privately, out of sight. The risks are all to me. They'd be mad not to take it'.

'You're assuming they'll be rational,' she says. 'No rational employer would have let things come this far; but, they did. Reasonable employers would have stood up by now and apologised; but, they haven't. They're neither rational, nor reasonable'.

'Hmm,' I sigh.

'They're not interested in doing the right things, or the amicable things,' she continues. 'They're only interested in getting their way, by any means it takes. They regard the law and the procedures of the land as things to be gotten around. They're quite happy to swear sincerely to tell the truth and then, proceed to lie blatantly. They think the law's there to control everyone else, while they get around it and do whatever they want. They're arrogant, shameless, and belligerent. They believe they're untouchable. They thought you could never win against them. You're the first employee they've not managed to quash, the first to hold them to account. The tribunal's decision against them only riles them. My advice is, forget reinstatement, save your money'.

~ Friday 15th December 2006, 1:30 p.m. ~

'Mr Singh, do you choose reinstatement or compensation?' the chairman asks me starting the reconvened remedy hearing.

'I choose reinstatement,' I answer firmly from my seat in the public gallery immediately behind my counsel.

Murmurs expressing surprise emanate from the public spectators sitting behind me. Neil and Simon stare at each other in astonishment.

The chairman looks at my counsel and signals her to speak.

'Mr Singh,' she begins, 'wishes to be reinstated in the Market Risk Controller role from which he is dismissed. In the event that the respondents cannot reinstate him in this role, then he wishes to be reinstated in one of the two vacancies he has seen advertised on the bank's website, both of which he is suited for'.

'The first,' she continues, 'is a Market Risk Associate role. It is in the Market Risk Control team in which Mr Singh worked. The role reports into Miss Mykonola, the retained Controller. Mr Singh informs me the role is vacant because the previous incumbent, Anthony Grenfell, who used to report into him, and with whom he still maintains contact, resigned and left the respondents' employment recently to take up employment at another financial institution. If the respondents cannot, for some reason, reinstate Mr Singh in his original Controller role, then he wishes to be reinstated in this Associate vacancy'.

'The second vacancy,' she continues, 'is the Risk Reporter role. This vacancy is in the Market Risk Reporting team, being the other team in the Market Risk Department that reports into Mr Hobson. In the event that the respondents cannot reinstate Mr Singh either in his Controller role or in the Associate role, then he wishes to be reinstated in this Risk Reporter vacancy. I have no more to say'.

Addressing the respondents' counsel, the chairman asks, 'will the respondents reinstate Mr Singh in the Controller role, or in one of the other two vacancies he identifies?'

She turns around and confers in private whispers with Neil, Simon, and Veronica, sitting immediately behind her. Reinstatement will solve all of my problems, and theirs. Entertaining high hopes of a positive, mutually beneficial decision, I await their answer with bated breath.

Finishing conferring, she turns around and answers,

'no, Sir. The respondents will not reinstate Mr Singh in any of those roles, nor in any other role'.

Huh! The absolute negativity and hardness of their resolve, to a remedy so amicable and so mutually beneficial, shocks me to the core. The reality it suddenly awakens me to petrifies me that they have no intention of behaving reasonably and cannot care less for facing up to their responsibilities. The decision disappoints me excessively, dashing my hopes for a prompt end to litigation and a cordial closure to this entire affair. I must armour up again and go back into battle.

'What is their reason for the refusal?' the chairman asks.

She turns around again, confers with the three of them in private whispers again, and then replies, 'the respondents will not reinstate Mr Singh in any role because he litigated against them'.

What? Really? They decline to reinstate me because I litigated against them? Whispers expressing shock and horror emanate from the spectators sitting in the public gallery. I tried my damnedest to avoid litigation. I gave them every opportunity to resolve the issues privately, and pre-empt the need to escalate matters to the courts. They sent me packing, leaving me no choice, but to litigate. How arrogant and conceited they are. They do me wrongs, then they do not give me any form of satisfactory closure, and now, they hold against me that I brought them to account? They push me down and expect me to just stay lying down and take it? This is utterly ridiculous. This cannot possibly be right. How brazen they are to declare boldly before the tribunal, and everyone present, this is their reason for refusal.

Appearing flabbergasted, as if he has never before heard such a reason, the chairman says sternly, 'while the respondents are entitled to decline reinstatement, they cannot rely on the reason that he litigated against them! The reason is unlawful! It is victimisation against him on the grounds of race! Would the respondents care to reconsider their reason?'

She turns around again and confers with all three of them, again. Shortly, she turns back around and answers, 'the respondents will not reinstate Mr Singh because reinstatement is *not possible*'.

'Very well,' the chairman says. 'The hearing may proceed on the basis that reinstatement is not possible. Who will give evidence on behalf of the respondents?'

'Simon Ong, the Director of the Market Risk Department,' she replies.

2

PROVISIONAL INTENTION

~ Friday 15th December 2006, 2:30 p.m. ~

'Mr Ong, is that your signature on the witness statement and is that the evidence you wish to give?' the respondents' counsel asks him.

He has just sworn in at the witness desk, positioned between the two counsels' desks and directly before the judges' bench. The three judges look down at him sitting isolated and exposed. He has presented the tribunal his statement on why my reinstatement is impossible. It says the following:

> Prior to Ranjit Singh's dismissal, there used to be two Market Risk Controller positions at the bank, each with a subordinate Market Risk Associate position reporting into it. Ranjit occupied one Controller position, and Katia Mykonola the other. The Controller role that he occupied was made redundant upon his dismissal. It no longer exists. Katia occupies the remaining role. The two subordinate Market Risk Associate roles both report into her now. It is impossible to reinstate Ranjit in a Controller role because the bank does not have a Controller vacancy available.
>
> My Market Risk Department is under huge financial pressures, requiring me to keep costs steady year-on-year. My main expenditure is on staff salaries and bonuses. The pressure on costs means I have to fund annual pay increases by reducing headcount or replacing expensive

employees with cheaper ones. The pressures preclude the resurrection of the redundant Controller role. This makes it impossible to create a Controller vacancy to reinstate Ranjit into. Furthermore, there is not enough work in the team for two Controllers.

It is impossible to reinstate Ranjit in another role that is commensurate with his level of seniority because the department does not have any such vacancy within his areas of expertise. Due to pressures on costs, the department is not in a position to be able to create a fresh role suitable for him to be reinstated into.

He is too senior for the Market Risk Associate role. The role reports into Katia, his peer. His level of seniority clashes with hers. His reinstatement in the Associate role below her will disrupt the workplace balance. Neil is still the person into whom the Market Risk Control team reports. So, the Associate role reports into him, albeit indirectly via Katia. The fact that Ranjit litigated against Neil means any situation where he reports into him, whether directly or indirectly, is impossible to work. For all these reasons, it is impossible to reinstate Ranjit into the Associate vacancy.

The Risk Reporter role reports directly into Neil. The role's focus is on risk *reporting*, which is different from the risk *analysis* focus of the Controller role that Ranjit performed. Ranjit does not possess the prerequisite understanding of reporting systems required for the Risk Reporter position. He is incapable of performing the role. The salary for the role is significantly lower than the salary he commanded as a Controller. For all these reasons, it is impossible to reinstate Ranjit into the vacancy.

'Yes,' he replies.

Addressing the chairman, the respondents' counsel says, 'I wish to bring up some supplementary issues, Sir'.

The chairman signals her to do so.

'Into whom does the Risk Reporter role report?' she asks Simon.

'Neil,' he answers.

'What is your view on Ranjit's suitability to the role?' she asks.

'The Risk Reporter role is very different to the Controller role Ranjit held,' he answers. 'The difference in the salaries for the roles reflects this. The Risk Reporter role focuses on *reporting* risks, not on *analysing* them, which is what the Controller role focuses on. It calls for a good understanding of reporting techniques and systems. Ranjit doesn't have that knowledge and understanding'.

'I have no more questions,' she says giving way to my counsel to begin her cross-examination.

'You have previously operated the Market Risk Control team with just two people, the two Controllers,' my counsel says.

'That's correct,' he replies. 'When the Head of Market Risk Control left in August 2004, the team continued to operate with just the two remaining members, Ranjit and Katia'.

'You operate the team with only Ranjit and Katia for six months,' she says.

'I can't remember,' he replies.

'The team *can* operate with just two Controllers,' she says.

'Although we managed back then,' he replies, 'operating the team with only two people is difficult and risky. There's the risk that when one is away on annual leave, the other might fall ill. Then, there'll be no cover in the team. I need at least three people in the team to ensure continuity of service. So, when the Head of Market

Risk Control left, I decided to mitigate the risk of the team again being in the position of fewer than three people by increasing the number to four. Rather than recruit another person to replace the departed Head, I decided to make the Head role redundant by reallocating his responsibilities to the two Controllers. I decided to create two new roles subordinate to the Controllers, the Associate roles, to whom some of the Controllers' simpler responsibilities would be reallocated'.

'After Ranjit's dismissal, the team operated with three individuals: Katia, the retained Controller; and Mary and Anthony, the two Associates,' she says.

'That's correct,' he replies.

'Anthony recently resigned and vacated his Associate position,' she says, 'leaving the team now manned by only two individuals'.

'Yes,' he replies.

'You say a team of fewer than three individuals is difficult and risky to operate,' she says.

'That's correct,' he replies. 'Three are needed to maintain proper operation'.

'You intend to fill the Associate vacancy to bring the number of individuals in the team back up to three,' she says.

'Yes,' he confirms.

'Ranjit's reinstatement as a Controller brings the number of individuals in the team back up to three,' she says. 'A restructured team of two Controllers and one Associate *can* be operated'.

'The restructure you're proposing is inefficient,' he replies. 'It will lead to spare capacity in the team'.

'Is optimising efficiency your main priority?' she asks.

'Yes,' he replies.

'If optimum efficiency is irrelevant, then the proposed team structure is perfectly feasible,' she says.

'I don't know what you mean,' he replies.

'I mean it will work,' she says.

'Er, yes, it'll work,' he replies, 'but it'll be inefficient because the team will be over-skilled'.

'It will work,' she asserts.

'Er, yes, it will work,' he confirms.

'Moving on,' she says. 'Ranjit is no longer employed at the bank. He is an outsider. By browsing the bank's public website, he manages to identify two reinstatement opportunities for himself, the Market Risk Associate and the Risk Reporter vacancy. You, on the other hand, are an insider. You are privy to more information about vacancies. Did you make any effort to look for potential reinstatement opportunities for him?'

'I'm not aware of any opportunities outside of my department,' he replies.

'You did not even bother to look,' she puts to him.

'No,' he confirms, 'I didn't look'.

'You say Ranjit does not possess the prerequisite knowledge to be able to perform the Risk Reporter role,' she says. 'Do you agree the Risk Reporter role is easier than the Controller role?'

'Er, I wouldn't say it's easier,' he replies. 'It's different. The Controller role requires a high level of understanding of financial instruments and risks. It requires hard technical knowledge to be able to make risk related decisions. It also requires soft skills to be able to liaise with the FSA and other stakeholders. The Risk Reporter role doesn't require all those skills'.

'Ranjit can perform the Risk Reporter role quite comfortably,' she puts to him.

'No, he can't,' he asserts.

'Neil, his line manager, provides the tribunal a list of jobs that he sees advertised at other financial institutions,' she says. 'He says all the jobs listed are suitable for Ranjit and that he should have applied for them to try to get another job following his dismissal. The list includes a number of Risk Reporter roles focusing on risk *reporting*. Neil seems to be saying Ranjit can perform roles that focus on risk reporting'.

'All of those roles are different to the Risk Reporter vacancy at hand,' he replies.

'Neil's evidence suggests Ranjit can be considered for the Risk Reporter role at hand,' she puts to him.

'Er,' he stalls. 'I suppose he can be *considered*, but he's not capable of performing it'.

'Neil's evidence suggests he is very capable of performing it,' she says.

'Maybe he can perform it, then,' he says indifferently.

The chairman interjects, 'Mr Ong! Answer the question properly! Is he or is he not capable of performing the role?'

'Er, hmm,' he stalls. 'He is,' he concedes reluctantly.

'Moving on,' my counsel says. 'You say the cost pressure your department is under makes Ranjit's reinstatement impossible'.

'Yes,' he replies firmly.

'The bank's annual bonus scheme is wholly discretionary, is it not?' she asks.

'Yes,' he answers.

'The payment of bonuses is not mandatory, is it?' she asks.

'No, it's not mandatory, it's completely discretionary,' he confirms. 'It's entirely up to the bank how much it wants to pay people. It doesn't have to pay people bonuses at all, if it doesn't want to'.

'In your previous testimony at the discrimination liability hearing, you testified that the bank paid out bonuses totalling *three million pounds* to fifty-five members of your staff for the year 2005,' she says.

'Yes,' he confirms.

'This three million pounds figure does not include your bonus, does it?' she asks.

'No, it doesn't,' he confirms.

'The 2005 bonus schedules disclosed to the tribunal show that you awarded some individuals bonuses of *one hundred and fifty thousand pounds* each,' she says.

'That's correct,' he confirms.

'You will award similar sized amounts for the forthcoming round of 2006 bonuses,' she says.

'I don't know yet,' he replies.

'The 2005 bonus schedules do not include details of bonuses paid to all of your staff members,' she says. 'The bonuses of the more senior members of your department, the heads of your teams, are excluded'.

'That's right,' he confirms. 'They're not included. Only the bonuses of band C and band D employees are disclosed because Ranjit was a band C employee'.

'Is it reasonable to say you awarded your heads of teams amounts even greater than one hundred and fifty thousand pounds each, because they are more senior members of your staff?' she asks.

'Yes,' he confirms.

'You are the most senior person in the department,' she says.

'Yes,' he confirms.

'Your bonus for 2005 is even higher,' she asserts.

'Er,' he stalls. 'Yes,' he confirms.

'When the bank is able to pay out wholly discretionary bonuses of such high magnitudes, clearly cost pressure is not really so great that the bank cannot afford to resurrect the redundant Controller role,' she puts to him.

'Er,' he mumbles. 'Those were last year's bonuses. They're history. Bonuses are entirely discretionary and aren't guaranteed from one year to the next. We don't know what will be paid for 2006'.

'Oh!' she says in sarcastic tone. 'So, you are not expecting a bonus for 2006, then?'

'Er,' he hesitates. 'Er, I am expecting one'.

'Of course, you are,' she says. 'What is your 2005 bonus award?'

'Er,' he stalls. 'Do I *really* need to answer that?'

The chairman interjects, 'answer the question, Mr Ong'.

'Hmm,' he hesitates. 'Six hundred thousand pounds,' he answers.

Mutterings expressing astonishment emanate from the spectators in the public gallery.

'*Six hundred thousand pounds*,' my counsel echoes his answer. 'Is that on top of your annual salary?' she asks.

'Yes,' he confirms.

'Do you expect a similar sized bonus for 2006?' she asks.

'Yes,' he answers.

'Moving on,' she says. 'You say any situation where Ranjit reports into Neil, whether directly or indirectly, is impossible to work'.

'That's right,' he confirms.

'Is Neil professional?' she asks.

'Yes, he is,' he replies.

'Is Ranjit professional?' she asks.

'Yes,' he replies.

'Despite both of them being professional,' she says, 'you claim Ranjit cannot return to work under Neil'.

'Er,' he stalls. 'Er, the situation would be difficult'.

'Before, you said it would be *impossible*, not *difficult*,' she says.

'Yes,' he confirms.

'Whatever the practicalities might be, you do not want to reinstate Ranjit because a situation where he somehow reports into Neil is impossible to work,' she says.

'Er, well, I, too, as the manager of the department, am concerned,' he replies.

The chairman interjects, 'Mr Ong, you evaded the question. Answer the question put to you!'

'Er, hmm, honestly speaking, I don't want him back in my department,' he admits.

'Is the reason you do not want him back because he litigated against Neil?' my counsel resumes.

'Er, the working relationship between them won't be effective,' he replies. 'He'll find working under Neil very difficult'.

'Who causes you concerns, Ranjit or Neil?' she asks.

'Ranjit,' he answers.

'If Ranjit is willing freely to return and work under Neil, then that should assure you and allay your concerns,' she says.

'Er, hmm,' he stalls. 'Er, I'm also concerned about Neil. He too might find Ranjit working under him difficult'.

'Why should Neil find Ranjit working under him difficult?' she asks.

'Er,' he contemplates, 'because he litigated against him. He named him personally as a respondent to the case. He accused him of race discrimination. Although the tribunal found Neil was unfair and discriminatory, Neil doesn't feel he's done anything wrong'.

'Are legal proceedings the issue?' she asks.

'Er, maybe not,' he answers, 'but the accusations Ranjit made are very personal to Neil'.

'Is the reason you do not want to reinstate Ranjit because he made an allegation of race discrimination?' she asks.

'Er,' he stalls. 'The relationship between them is not conducive to an effective working environment,' he answers.

The chairman intervenes, 'Mr Ong, you evaded the question again! You are being asked if the reason you do not want to reinstate Mr Singh is because he made and sustained an allegation of race discrimination against Mr Hobson. Answer this question!'

'Er,' he stalls again. 'Hmm,' he hesitates. 'Yes, that is the reason,' he concedes finally.

'I have no more questions,' my counsel says.

The chairman invites the respondents' counsel to re-examine him.

'Is it possible to operate the Market Risk Control team with two Controllers and one Associate?' she asks.

'It's not impossible,' he answers, 'but it would mean we have two highly skilled individuals supported by one junior person, which is not a good configuration to get the work done efficiently'.

'Now that there is only one Controller and one Associate in the team,' she says, 'could you reconfigure the team to be comprised of two Controllers and one Associate?'

'I made it very clear in my previous testimony that we looked at our requirements during the redundancy exercise and decided the correct configuration is one Controller and two Associates,' he replies. 'We can reconfigure the team in other ways, but they won't match our needs'.

'I have no further questions,' she says.

'Mr Ong,' the chairman says, 'you claim your department is under huge financial pressure requiring you to keep costs steady year-on-year. To what extent does natural wastage, like voluntary resignations, account for the required cost savings?'

'Er, I don't know,' he answers.

'Surely, Mr Ong,' the chairman says, 'some of your staff must resign and move on; it is normal'.

'Yes,' he confirms.

'What percentage is that, on an annual basis?' the chairman asks.

'The rate of natural staff attrition is usually about ten per cent,' he answers. 'But, in active years, it can be twenty per cent'.

'Can the required cost savings be achieved by natural staff attrition?' the chairman asks.

'Hmm, yes,' he answers, 'if I don't replace some of the leavers'.

'Some of the leavers would need replacing,' the chairman says.

'Yes,' he replies.

'But, not all of them,' the chairman says, 'because sometimes you can reorganise work so some of your remaining members of staff can step up to take on more responsibilities, like you did when the Head of Market Risk Control left'.

'Er, yes, that's correct,' he confirms. 'I don't need to replace each and every leaver'.

'You are released, Mr Ong,' the chairman says. 'You may leave the witness stand'.

~~~

The chairman signals my counsel to present my case on reinstatement.

'Reinstatement is the primary legal remedy for an unfair dismissal,' my counsel starts. 'Mr Singh identifies a role for the purpose, the Market Risk Controller role from which he is dismissed. There is no reason why a restructured team of two Controllers and one Associate will not work. Mr Ong accepts the proposed restructure is practical, although not optimally efficient. The priority in considering reinstatement is *practicality*, not optimum *efficiency*. Reinstatement will work'.

'Moving on to the matter of reinstatement in other roles,' she continues. 'Mr Singh identifies two vacancies, the Market Risk Associate vacancy and the Risk Reporter vacancy. The Market Risk Associate role reports into Mr Hobson indirectly, and the Risk Reporter role reports into him directly. The only reason Mr Ong effectively gives against reinstatement in these two vacancies is because Mr Singh litigated against Mr Hobson with an allegation of race discrimination. The reason is unlawful. It constitutes victimisation against Mr Singh on the grounds of race. Again, reinstatement will work'.

'In the circumstances, the tribunal should order the respondents to reinstate Mr Singh in the Market Risk Controller role,' she submits, 'or, alternatively, in either the Market Risk Associate or the Risk Reporter vacancy'.

~~~

The chairman signals the respondents' counsel to present their case on reinstatement.

'Although a reconfigured Market Risk Control team of two Controllers and one Associate will work,' the respondents' counsel starts, 'it will not work at optimum efficiency. The team has, at times, comprised of only two Controllers. But, it has never comprised of two Controllers and one Associate. There is not enough work in the team to keep two Controllers occupied. The department is under huge financial pressure. Clearly, reinstatement is impossible'.

'Moving on to the matter of reinstatement in other roles,' she continues. 'The relationship between Mr Singh and Mr Hobson is unworkable. The reason for the unworkable relationship is nothing to do with the fact that Mr Singh litigated against Mr Hobson with an allegation of race discrimination. It is because Mr Singh fails to accept Mr Hobson's authority during the course of his employment under him'.

'In the circumstances,' she continues, 'reinstating Mr Singh is impossible. The tribunal must not order reinstatement'.

The chairman interjects, 'you submit Mr Singh fails to accept Mr Hobson's authority whilst he worked under him. Unfairly dismissed employees rarely opt for reinstatement. But, Mr Singh does. Underlying his choice, there is a duty of faith on his part to make reinstatement under Mr Hobson work. Mr Ong, a third party, expresses concerns over the practicality of the relationship. But, the tribunal notes that Mr Hobson, the actual person in the relationship, does not come forth himself and testify the relationship is unworkable. Furthermore, the respondents do not submit formally to the tribunal that Mr Hobson says he cannot make Mr Singh's reinstatement under himself work'.

She turns around and confers with Neil in private whispers.

Upon finishing conferring, she answers, 'Mr Hobson advises me he cannot see any situation working in which he manages Mr Singh. The tribunal should take this into consideration and must not order reinstatement. Clearly, Mr Hobson is in a very difficult position because Mr Singh named him personally as a respondent in litigation'.

'Hmm,' the chairman contemplates. 'Do continue with the remainder of your submission,' he says.

'I have no more to submit,' she replies.

'Very well,' the chairman says. Addressing both counsels, he continues, 'the hearing is adjourned for the tribunal to consider the evidence and make its decision. It is three-thirty now. All parties are to reconvene for four-thirty for the tribunal's decision'.

~ Friday 15th December 2006, 4:30 p.m. ~

We are all gathered before the tribunal to receive its decision on ordering reinstatement. I sit in my regular spot in the public gallery immediately behind my counsel, on the far right hand side of the courtroom. As usual, Neil, Simon, Veronica, and the bank's other officers sit together in the public gallery immediately behind their counsel, on the far left hand side of the room. The public gallery is full with spectators. With no expectation of a decision in my favour, considering my counsel's pessimistic prediction and clear advice, but with the keenest eagerness to know the tribunal's reasons, I brace myself to receive its decision.

'Upon establishing Mr Singh is unfairly dismissed,' the chairman starts, 'the tribunal explained the available remedies to him. He wishes to be reinstated in the Market Risk Controller role from which is dismissed. He also expresses that if reinstatement in the Controller role is not possible, then, in the alternative, he wishes to be reinstated in the vacant Market Risk Associate or the Risk Reporter role'.

'The respondents cannot,' the chairman continues, 'rely on Mr Singh's act of litigating against them as a basis for impossibility of reinstatement, because it is an unlawful basis, being victimisation on the grounds of race'.

'The tribunal is required,' the chairman continues, 'to consider whether Mr Singh causes his own dismissal, or contributes to it in anyway. As the respondents make no suggestions whatsoever to this effect, the tribunal concludes the matter simply does not arise'.

'The tribunal can, therefore, move on to the matter of whether reinstatement is possible,' the chairman says. 'The respondents say reinstating Mr Singh is impossible due to two factors: the structure of the Market Risk Control team; and Mr Singh's relationship with Mr Hobson'.

'The team structure, of one Controller and two Associates,' the chairman continues, 'is the consequence of Mr Hobson's desire to dismiss Mr Singh unlawfully. Mr Hobson testified that if, after informing the other team members that their jobs are safe, he reconsidered Mr Singh's dismissal and found someone else ought to be dismissed instead, then he would retain Mr Singh and dismiss the other person. Mr Ong testified the same. The respondents submitted the same. It is clearly evident that the team structure can be revised according to requirements. Clearly, the team structure, as it stands following Mr Singh's dismissal, is not a factor that amounts to impossibility, neither in isolation, nor when combined with any financial pressure the department might be under. If Mr Singh is reinstated, then the respondents will have to face up to any knock on effects there might be on the team structure'.

'Turing now to the relationship between Mr Hobson and Mr Singh,' the chairman continues. 'The bank says it is *Mr Singh* who is unable to make reinstatement under Mr

Hobson work, not the other way around. The tribunal notes the cause of Mr Singh's dismissal is the manner in which *Mr Hobson* relates to him, not the way he relates to Mr Hobson. The consequences of Mr Hobson's manner are relatively insignificant upon himself, compared to those upon Mr Singh. He has merely had to appear in a court of law to give his testimony and undergo cross-examination. Mr Singh, on the other hand, has lost his job, his income, and, possibly, his career too. In the circumstances, if anyone has a right to feel aggrieved, then it is Mr Singh. Yet still, he is ready and willing to return to work for the respondents, and even to work under Mr Hobson. The tribunal acknowledges his readiness includes a willingness to serve under Mr Hobson faithfully, and to answer to him'.

'Some events that were aired during the liability hearing might make the relationship difficult,' the chairman continues. 'Mr Hobson and Mr Singh may well have to put them in the past and draw a line under them in order to move on and work together. However, the fact that a relationship might be difficult is insufficient to render reinstatement impossible'.

'In the circumstances,' the chairman continues, 'the respondents fail to satisfy the tribunal that reinstatement is impossible. The tribunal orders the respondents to reinstate Mr Singh in the Market Risk Controller role from which he is dismissed, or, alternatively, in either the Market Risk Associate or the Risk Reporter vacancy. The tribunal's decision is unanimous'.

Wonderful! The ruling thrills me. It is what I wanted. It gives me grounds for great optimism. Surely, no employer would go against the formal orders of a tribunal. Soon, litigation will be over and life will be reset to how it used to be.

My counsel twists around to face me. With a smile spread across her face, she gives me a double thumbs-up gesture. I read her lips mime, congratulations. I acknowledge her with a heartfelt return smile. The thought delights me that she can no longer say she has never managed to convince a tribunal to award reinstatement to any of her clients'.

Addressing the respondents' counsel, the chairman says, 'you may take instructions from the respondents on how they intend to respond to the reinstatement orders'.

She turns around and confers in private whispers with Neil, Simon, and Veronica.

They are going to comply with the orders, I tell myself with great optimism. They are going to reinstate me as a Controller. I await their response with bated breath.

Upon finishing conferring, she replies, 'the respondents provisionally indicate an intention to comply with the order to reinstate Mr Singh in the Market Risk Controller role. As it is close to Christmas now, the earliest feasible reinstatement date is Monday the 8th of January. Mr Singh should report to work at nine o'clock in the morning'.

'*Provisionally indicate an intention to comply*,' the chairman echoes her words. 'The order is unenforceable,' he continues. 'The respondents my go away and take some time to consider the matter and return before the tribunal to give their final decision, on Wednesday the 3rd of January. If their decision turns out to be negative, then they are to present the tribunal with *further* and *better* arguments on why compliance with the orders is impossible, than the two they essentially rely on so far'.

3

LONG WAY SHORT

~ Wednesday 3rd January 2007, 11:00 a.m. ~

'I do solemnly, sincerely and truly declare and affirm that the evidence I shall give shall be the truth the whole truth and nothing but the truth,' Neil swears sitting isolated at the witness desk positioned between the two counsels and before the judges' bench.

I sit in my regular spot, in the public gallery, directly behind my counsel. I have a clear side on view of him. To my great disappointment, the respondents decided not to reinstate me. Neil has presented the tribunal his statement on why compliance with the reinstatement orders is impossible. It says the following:

> Following Ranjit Singh's dismissal, the work in the Market Risk Control team is carried out successfully with just one Market Risk Controller supported by two Market Risk Associates. There is not enough work in the team to sustain the alternative structure he proposes of two Controllers supported by one Associate. The amount of work the team performs requires one Controller and two Associates, not two Controllers and one Associate. During the course of Ranjit's employment, one Associate reported into him, and the other into Katia Mykonola. Following his dismissal, they both report into Katia, the retained Controller. Never before has an Associate reported into two Controllers, which is what he now proposes. The team has never operated with

the structure he suggests.

I spoke with Katia and Mary Richardson, the remaining Associate, about the structure Ranjit proposes of two Controllers and one Associate. They both say the structure will not work in practice because it can lead to situations where the two Controllers give conflicting instructions to the Associate. Katia says she is extremely worried about the possibility of this because Ranjit is not an easy person to work with. Both Katia and Mary say they have grave concerns about the potential impact on the team's efficiency and credibility arising out of possible differences of opinions between the Controllers, which could place the Associate in difficult situations. They both say they will be very unhappy if a second Controller is now introduced into the team.

Whilst Katia accepts challenging management and the risk processes is part of the Controllers' job description, she now tells me she finds Ranjit is excessive in his level of challenge. She says she has to spend too much time and energy in meetings with him to explain why decisions are being made as they are, in order to try to convince him to agree with the rationales behind them. She says she does not feel the working relationship between them is as efficient as it ought to be.

Katia says she is also extremely concerned that Ranjit's relationship with me does not work because she believes he has many issues with me as his manager. She says she was aware from the moment she joined the team that he constantly challenges my authority and my remit as his manager. She says this was an issue throughout the time she worked in the team with him. She says the issues he has with not accepting me as his manager are clearly unresolved at the time of his dismissal. She says his reinstatement under me will not work because the issues still persist. She says his reinstatement is not conducive to a good working environment, and there cannot be an effective working relationship between him and me.

I too hold the view that Ranjit's reluctance to accept me as his manger effectively precludes reinstatement as a possible remedy. I am of the view that if he is reinstated, then he will continue to have issues with my authority, as he did previously over the two years of his employment under me. He is a tenacious man who does not let matters drop. Whilst I appreciate he expresses a wish to be reinstated and indicates he will be happy to work under me again, I am of the opinion that it just will not be possible in practical terms, given the issues he has with my authority. I do not believe, even with the best will in the world, the relationship between us can be such that we can work together effectively. He has had issues with my authority ever since I was appointed his manager. I see no reason to believe this will change upon his reinstatement. Reinstatement will place me in a position where I cannot do my work because most of my time will be spent dealing with his issues regarding my authority.

Katia and Mary are not available to appear before the tribunal to testify in person on their own behalves because they are both on annual leave and are away abroad.

Katia is away visiting her mother, who lives in Greece and is very seriously ill. Although she discussed her views about Ranjit's reinstatement with me, she does not feel she is in a position to be able to give a written witness statement due to pressing issues in her personal life. She cannot cope with the additional stress of having to give a statement and of being called to appear before the tribunal in person to be cross-examined.

I spoke with Mary also and discussed whether she has any issues surrounding Ranjit's reinstatement. She never worked for Ranjit directly. Therefore, she can only comment in general terms about the proposed alternative team structure. She too is very stressed about the prospect of giving a written witness statement. In the end, Simon Ong and I, in consultation with Veronica Cotton, our department's HR Partner, decided a written witness statement would not be adduced from her because she never reported into Ranjit directly.

Ranjit's reinstatement in the vacant Market Risk Associate and the Risk Reporter role is also impossible because he will be reporting into me, indirectly and directly, respectively, and because he is too senior for the roles.

'Mr Hobson, is that your signature on the witness statement and is that the evidence you wish to give?' the respondents' counsel asks him.

'Yes,' he replies.

She gives way to my counsel to begin her cross-examination.

'Have you spoken with Katia and Mary about the statements you give here today on their behalves?' my counsel asks.

'Yes, I have,' he answers.

'The tribunal is not supplied any independent evidence, such as statements with their signatures on, showing they agree with the testimony you give on their behalves,' she says.

'No,' he confirms. 'Er, but,' he adds, 'they both sent me emails confirming they agree with what I say on their behalves'.

'You do not disclose the emails to the tribunal,' she says.

'Er,' he stalls. 'No,' he confirms. 'But, also,' he adds, his hands shaking, 'I spoke with both of them in the presence of my legal counsel. She witnessed their agreements to the testimonies I give on their behalves. She can confirm that they agree with what I say for them'.

'Katia's mother's illness is known about for some years now,' she says.

'Yes, that's correct,' he confirms.

'There is no particular or sudden crisis right now that necessitates an urgent visit by Katia,' she asserts.

'That's correct,' he replies. 'She visits her whenever she can'.

'The level of stress Katia experiences is not so great, and the issues in her personal life are not so pressing, that she is prevented from leading a normal working life,' she puts to him.

'Er,' he stalls. 'Yes, that's correct'.

'She was born in Greece and is forty-three years old,' she says.

'Yes,' he confirms.

'She comes to England alone as a teenager to study A Levels at school,' she says.

'That's correct,' he replies.

'She has a First Class Honours degree in Mathematical Physics from a London university,' she says.

'That's correct,' he confirms.

'She has a Ph.D. in Mathematics from another London university,' she says.

'That's correct,' he says.

'She has worked in some very high-profile, senior roles at a number of top-tier financial institutions in the City,' she says.

'Yes, that's correct,' he replies.

'She is a high-powered, strong-minded, capable,

professional woman,' she asserts.

'Yes,' he confirms.

'She cannot be so stressed that she cannot provide the tribunal a written witness statement of her own views before going away,' she puts to him.

'She was so stressed,' he says.

'The reason why you do not bring her here to testify in person before the tribunal, and expose her to cross-examination, is because she does not support your views. Her testimony will undermine the case you make against complying with the reinstatement orders,' she says.

'That's incorrect,' he replies. 'She supports my views'.

'Mary too is a high-powered, strong-minded, professional woman,' she puts to him.

'Yes,' he confirms.

'She too cannot be so stressed that she cannot provide a written witness statement of her own views before going away,' she says.

'She was so stressed,' he asserts.

'The reason why you do not bring her, either, to testify in person is also because she does not support your views. Her testimony, too, will undermine the case you make against reinstatement,' she says.

'That's incorrect,' he replies. 'She, too, supports my views. I've already said,' he reiterates, 'I spoke with both of them in the presence of my legal counsel. She can confirm they agree with what I say on their behalves'.

'You have a vested interest in the outcome of the matter of reinstatement,' she says. 'In the absence of any independent witness statements from Katia and Mary, and of any other independent evidence, the tribunal has only your word that they support your views'.

'Yes,' he replies.

'You say they both express there is a possibility of the Associate being put in difficult positions by differences of opinions between two Controllers,' she says.

'Yes,' he confirms.

'The concern can be pre-empted in practice quite easily by having Mary continue to report into Katia only, and accept instructions from her exclusively, while Ranjit works in the team without support from her,' she says.

'No, it can't,' he replies.

'Why not?' she asks.

'Because the team has never before been operated in such a way,' he answers.

'Moving on,' she says. 'Previously, you testified Ranjit gets on well with people at the bank, including Katia and Mary'.

'Er,' he stalls. 'That's right. Er, but I meant he gets on well generally, on a *personal* level. I didn't mean on a *professional* level also'.

'Never before have you said he is difficult to work with and does not get on professionally with Katia and Mary,' she says.

'Er, that's correct,' he replies, his hands shaking again. 'While my personal opinion is that they all get on well, Katia has now complained to me that working with Ranjit is difficult'.

'Actually, neither Katia nor Mary make any such complaint to you,' she puts to him.

'They do,' he rebuts.

The chairman interjects, 'Mr Hobson, is it correct that the nature of the work the Controllers perform is such that there is room for both of them to justifiably hold differing professional views on a particular subject?'

'Yes,' he confirms.

'Differing views, by themselves, do not necessarily signify they do not get on with each other professionally,' the chairman says. 'It is quite possible to have differing professional views and still get on well professionally'.

'Yes, that's correct,' he replies.

'Then, judging whether they get on professionally is a difficult task to perform,' the chairman says.

'Yes, that's right,' he agrees.

'For a moment,' the chairman says, 'put aside the matter of them getting on in a professional sense. Does anyone ever complain to you that Mr Singh does not get on with him or her in the more general and colloquial sense?'

'Er, no,' he answers.

'Now, let us return to the matter of getting on in a professional sense,' the chairman says. 'Do you agree there is a range of levels of intensity of not getting on in a professional sense? At one end of the range, the low intensity end, the individuals are still able to work together. At the opposite end, the high intensity end, the difficulties between them are so great that they are unable to work together at all'.

'Yes,' he agrees.

'In your experience,' the chairman continues, 'are you familiar with situations where people have had difficulties working together?'

'Yes,' he answers.

'Would you be able to judge whether the level between Mr Singh and Miss Mykonola reached a height where they experienced difficulties working together?' the chairman asks.

'Yes, I would be able to judge that,' he answers.

'Of course, you would,' the chairman says, 'because if the level ever reached such a difficult and unworkable intensity, then, as their manager, you would have to intervene and manage the difficulties between them'.

'Er, only if the difficulties are apparent to me,' he replies.

'Yes,' the chairman says. 'But, if such difficulties existed, then, of course, they would be apparent to you. They would manifest in their behaviours towards each other, in their email correspondences, oral communications, and other exchanges and interactions between them, all of which you, as their manager, would be privy to'.

'Er,' he contemplates. 'Hmm, yes,' he concedes.

'Clearly, you noticed no such difficulties,' the chairman says. 'Clearly, there were no such difficulties. Mr Singh and Miss Mykonola made their professional relationship work'.

'Er,' he mumbles. 'Yes,' he concedes reluctantly.

'Does the level ever get to a difficult or unworkable height at any time before Mr Singh's dismissal?' the chairman asks.

'No,' he answers.

'After his dismissal, does Katia inform you of any difficulties between them?' the chairman asks.

'She didn't inform me of any *difficulties*, as such,' he answers. 'But, she says decision-making is easier since his departure'.

'Obviously, she finds decision-making easier now,' the chairman asserts as a matter of fact. 'She now possesses the authority to make decisions single-handedly whereas before, she needed to make some decisions jointly with Mr Singh, which may have entailed some consultation and differing views'.

'Er, yes,' he agrees.

The chairman signals my counsel to continue.

'You and Katia may prefer the single-handed decision-making situation she now enjoys,' my counsel resumes, 'but the previous situation, in which some decisions were made jointly by Katia and Ranjit, worked well'.

'It worked,' he replies, 'but not well'.

'If Ranjit is reinstated, then a professional, workable relationship between him and Katia will ensue,' she says.

'Er, hmm,' he contemplates. 'Yes,' he concedes.

'If any issues arise in terms of them not getting on with each other, then you can manage them, just as you might have done before,' she puts to him.

'Er, yes,' he replies. 'But,' he adds, 'having to manage them is inefficient'.

'Inefficiency is irrelevant in complying with

reinstatement orders,' she asserts as a matter of fact. 'Neither Katia nor Mary make any complaint to you at any time prior to Ranjit's dismissal to the effect that he does not get on with them. You managed before, you will manage again'.

'Possibly,' he replies. 'Katia is the one to credit for making the situation between them work, not Ranjit,' he adds.

'Does Katia or Mary ever mention any issue to you?' she asks.

'I have no evidence of there being any issues,' he answers.

'Does anyone else ever suggest to you that there is a problem of Ranjit not getting on with anybody?' she asks.

'No,' he answers.

'Are there any remarks or notes on Ranjit's employment record that might evidence there is an issue?' she asks.

'No,' he answers.

'One scoring criteria used in the redundancy selection exercise you performed is, *"how the individual gets on with others",*' she continues. 'You award Ranjit the highest mark possible for this criteria. The redundancy scorecard, his performance appraisals, and his other official employment records all show that he gets on well with everyone. The records contradict the testimony you give here today'.

'Er,' he stalls. 'From my perspective there's no issue. I feel he has issues, though, with my authority as his manager'.

'Are you officially part of the Market Risk Control team?' she asks.

'Yes,' he answers.

'You provide the tribunal a one-page handwritten note, which you made in December 2005 regarding Ranjit's performance for the year,' she says.

'That's correct,' he replies.

She directs the tribunal to the handwritten note in the

bundles of evidence and then, asks him, 'is that your handwriting?'

'Yes,' he confirms.

'You wrote everything that is on that page?' she asks.

'Yes,' he confirms.

'You use this handwritten note later to complete Ranjit's 2005 year-end appraisal,' she says.

'That's correct,' he replies. 'I made the note during a meeting with Ranjit about his performance for the year. Later on, I used the note to write up his official appraisal'.

'The note shows you categorise your thoughts under the following subheadings: *Enjoyed*; *Direction*; *Achievements*; *Low Points*; and *Developments*,' she says. 'Under the subheading, Achievements, you write, *"Ranjit's working relationship with the Market Risk Control team members"*. You categorise his working relationship with the team as an achievement'.

'Er,' he stalls. 'Er, the things I categorised under, Achievements, are the things he told me of as being his achievements. They don't originate from me. Ranjit said they're achievements, but that doesn't mean they actually are achievements'.

'You do not disagree with him when he reports to you his working relationship with the team as an achievement,' she says. 'You note it down under, Achievements'.

'Er, that's right,' he confirms.

'The facts are: he has a good working relationship with the team, of which you consider yourself to be a member; and he has a good working relationship with you,' she says.

'Er, that's correct on some things,' he replies, 'but not on the subject of my authority as his manager'.

'Nathan Wilcox, the bank's Head of Fraud, investigated Ranjit's formal grievance about race discrimination,' she says. 'He interviews you as part of his investigation'.

'That's correct,' he confirms.

'The bank has presented the tribunal with the minutes of the interview, which are taken by an HR representative who was present,' she says.

'Yes,' he replies.

She directs the tribunal to the minutes in the bundles of evidence and then, says to Neil, 'the minutes show that you tell Nathan you have, *"a good working relationship with Ranjit"*.

'Er, yes, I did tell him that,' he confirms. 'But, Ranjit didn't accept me as his manager,' he adds.

'You do not tell Nathan that Ranjit does not accept you as his manager,' she says. 'You describe your relationship with Ranjit as being, *"a good working relationship"*.

'Er, hmm, yes, that's correct,' he concedes reluctantly.

'Prior to the remedies hearing, whenever you gave an account of your relationship with Ranjit, your account is the relationship is a good one,' she says. 'Only since the matter of his reinstatement coming into play, do you start suddenly suggesting he does not get on with you and does not accept you as his manager. You suggest this because you do not want him reinstated'.

'That's not so,' he replies.

'You put words that suit your purpose into Katia's and Mary's mouths by testifying on their behalves,' she says.

'I'm not putting words in their mouths,' he replies, his hands trembling. 'They both told my legal counsel they agree with what I'm saying on their behalves'.

'If there *really* were any working relationship issues in the team,' she says, 'then there would be some contemporaneous evidence to that effect, like remarks in his official performance appraisals, or other company records showing disciplinary actions taken against him'.

'Er, hmm,' he mumbles, his voice croaking and his knees also trembling now.

'There is no such contemporaneous evidence,' my counsel continues. 'The contemporaneous evidence shows the contrary, that he has *good* relationships with everyone'.

'Hmm,' he contemplates nervously.

'Your counsel, on the 15th of December, in her case against the making of reinstatement orders, submits to the tribunal, *"Clearly, Mr Hobson is in a very difficult position because Mr Singh named him personally as a respondent in litigation",*' she says. 'Clearly, the reason you do not want to reinstate Ranjit is because he litigated against you and alleged race discrimination'.

'No, that's incorrect,' he protests, but the strain across his face betrays him.

'What motivates you is that he litigated against you on the grounds of race,' she says.

'No,' he says, his whole body trembling.

'You made up your mind that you are not going to reinstate him because he litigated against you,' she says. 'You are now trying to get the evidence to fit your decision'.

'That's not so,' he says.

'I have no further questions,' she says.

Addressing the respondents' counsel, the chairman asks, 'do you wish to re-examine your witness?'

'No, Sir,' she answers. 'Er,' she hesitates. 'There is a matter I must address,' she adds in awkward tone.

'Oh? What is it?' the chairman asks.

'It is a matter that could impact my personal and professional reputation,' she says.

'Do go on,' the chairman says.

'It concerns Mr Hobson's testimony that he spoke with Miss Mykonola and Mrs Richardson in the presence of his legal counsel. It is incumbent on me to inform the tribunal that neither I, nor anyone else from my legal team, was ever present at any discussions that might have occurred between Mr Hobson, Miss Mykonola, and Mrs Richardson'.

Gasps and murmurs expressing shock and horror emanate from the spectators in the public gallery. Neil cringes at the witness stand.

'We have not been privy to any discussions that might

have occurred between them,' she continues. 'We are not in a position to be able to verify that Miss Mykonola and Mrs Richardson agree with the testimony Mr Hobson gives on their behalves'.

'Noted,' the chairman replies.

Neil quivers cowering isolated and exposed at the witness stand before the judges and the public.

'Mr Hobson,' the chairman says looking down at him, 'you are released. You may leave the witness stand'.

~~~

The chairman signals the respondents' counsel to present their case on why compliance with the reinstatement orders is impossible.

'On the subject of the alternative team structure Mr Singh proposes, of two Controllers and one Associate,' she starts, 'Mr Hobson proffers a business rationale for why the structure is impossible; it is because the structure has never been deployed before. The team structure of two Controllers and two Associates, which was in place prior to Mr Singh's dismissal, is now also impossible because there is not enough work in the team. It is important to note that Mr Hobson is not challenged on whether there is insufficient work in the team to sustain two Controllers'.

'Moving on,' she continues. 'Mr Hobson says Miss Mykonola and Mrs Richardson recently informed him that relationships within the team, and the team's efficiency, are better following Mr Singh's dismissal. Mr Singh is unable to accept Mr Hobson's authority over himself. Mr Singh's inability to accept Mr Hobson as his manager remains an issue for Mr Singh. If he is reinstated, then his inability to accept Mr Hobson's authority will continue to be an issue for him'.

'In conclusion,' she submits, 'compliance with the reinstatement orders is impossible'.

The chairman signals my counsel to present my case on why compliance with the reinstatement orders is possible.

'Mr Hobson decides from the outset not to reinstate Mr Singh,' she starts. 'Then, he tries to make the evidence fit his decision. The respondents' case against reinstatement has no credibility at all. It should be rejected'.

'The tribunal must ask itself why Miss Mykonola and Mrs Richardson do not provide any written witness statements expressing their own views?' she continues. 'The tribunal must also ask itself why the respondents do not supply any other forms of independent evidence from them showing what their views are? Mr Hobson says his legal counsel is witness to the fact that they agree with the testimony he gives on their behalves. His legal counsel says this is not the case. The tribunal must consider why his legal counsel intervenes on the testimony he gives and contradicts it? In the absence of independent evidence, the tribunal has no way of knowing the extent to which Miss Mykonola and Mrs Richardson agree with the testimony Mr Hobson gives on their behalves'.

'The fact that Mr Singh has good working relationships with everyone at work,' she continues, 'including Mr Hobson, is shown overwhelmingly by the contemporaneous evidence. It is evidenced by his official performance appraisals and by his redundancy scorecard, both being records Mr Hobson himself completes. It is also evidenced by the minutes of Mr Wilcox's interview of Mr Hobson'.

'The testimony Mr Hobson gives on behalf of Miss Mykonola and Mrs Richardson,' she continues, 'is blatantly false because the contemporaneous evidence clearly shows the contrary. The tribunal must ask itself if reinstatement is now impossible, then why is there no evidence to that effect prior to the matter of reinstatement coming into play?'

'The reason why the respondents do not reinstate Mr Singh is obvious,' she continues. 'They stated it openly at the start of the remedy hearing on the 15th of December. The reason is because Mr Singh litigated against them on the grounds of race'.

'From a business perspective,' she continues, 'there is enough work in the department for the respondents to reinstate Mr Singh'.

The chairman interjects, 'is reinstatement possible given that Mr Hobson says there is only enough work for one Controller and two Associates?'

'Mr Hobson does not provide any evidence to back up his word on the matter,' she answers. 'Therefore, reinstatement is possible'.

'Will it still remain possible if the tribunal decides to accept his word, even without any supporting evidence?' the chairman asks.

'Yes,' she answers. 'Even then, reinstatement remains possible because, as a Controller, Mr Singh can also perform the work of the Associate who left the team recently. Furthermore, the alternative team structure Mr Singh proposes is entirely feasible because it is very similar to a previous team structure. Feasibility signifies possibility'.

'Hmm,' the chairman reflects on her submission leaning back into his chair. He muses for a moment and then, sitting up again, signals her to continue.

'The respondents' claim, that the proposed structure is inefficient, is irrelevant because *efficiency* is not the correct test for the remedy of reinstatement,' she continues. 'The correct test is *possibility*. Mr Singh's reinstatement is quite possible because the proposed structure can be implemented quite feasibly. Any workplace disagreements between Miss Mykonola and Mr Singh can be managed and resolved, just as they might have been before. In conclusion, it is perfectly possible to comply with the tribunal's orders of reinstatement. I have no more to say'.

Addressing both counsels, the chairman says, 'the hearing is adjourned for the tribunal to consider the evidence and make its decision. It is now midday. All parties are to reconvene for two o'clock for the tribunal's decision'.

~ Wednesday 3rd January 2007, 2:00 p.m. ~

We are all gathered before the tribunal to receive its decision on whether compliance with its reinstatement orders is possible. I feel confident of a decision in my favour. But, what does it matter? The respondents refuse to reinstate me; the reinstatement orders cannot be enforced. The tribunal's decision will be an academic matter only, more for completeness of legal process, rather than of any meaningful practical application. Remedy will have to proceed to compensation, by default.

'Mr Singh's dismissal left the Market Risk Control team with one Controller and two Associates,' the chairman begins. 'One Associate role is now vacant because the incumbent, Mr Grenfell, left the respondents' employment recently'.

'When the tribunal issued its reinstatement orders, it took into account the possibility of the respondents complying with them,' the chairman continues. 'At the time, the tribunal was unconvinced that compliance is impossible'.

'Having not reinstated Mr Singh in accordance with the orders,' the chairman continues, 'the respondents bring upon themselves the burden of proving compliance is impossible. Their argument in the discharge of the burden is essentially twofold; there is a *commerciality* aspect, and one of *personality*'.

'First, the tribunal considers the commerciality aspect,' the chairman says.

'It would be wrong to place the respondents in a position of significant over-manning of their operations,' the chairman continues. 'Mr Ong testifies that running the team with Mr Singh's suggested alternative structure, of two Controllers and one Associate, is possible. He makes the case that he wishes to retain three individuals in the team. His reason is because if one team member is absent due to sickness whilst another is away on annual leave, then the team will still be manned by the third. Retaining three individuals in the team is exactly what is being considered under reinstatement. Reinstatement does not amount to significant over-manning of operations'.

'On the matter of the amount of work there is in the team,' the chairman continues, 'Mr Hobson claims there is not enough work to sustain two Controllers and one Associate, as opposed to one Controller and two Associates. He does not back up his claim with any specific evidence. When he selected Mr Singh for dismissal, he provided the bank's union with very detailed analytical evidence showing how Mr Singh's workload can be reallocated amongst one Controller and two Associates. He does not present any satisfactory evidence now showing the team's workload cannot be reallocated amongst two Controllers and one Associate. Meanwhile, he actively seeks to fill the Associate vacancy'.

'Moving on to Mr Singh's suggestion that the respondents can set up the team structure so the remaining Associate continues to report into, and be managed by, Miss Mykonola exclusively, as opposed to taking instructions from the two of them,' the chairman continues. 'The suggestion is entirely feasible. It benefits Mrs Richardson in terms of consistency of instructions and continuity. It also enables some of the additional workload that is currently upon her, as a result of Mr Grenfell's departure, to be reallocated to Mr Singh upon his reinstatement'.

'Regarding the matter of the financial pressure the

Market Risk Department is under,' the chairman continues. 'Given the level of wholly discretionary bonus awards the bank seems to be able to afford to pay, the tribunal finds very difficult to understand how Mr Ong can sustain his claim that the cost pressure on the department is so great that Mr Singh's reinstatement is rendered impossible from an economic aspect'.

'Moving on now to the personalities aspect,' the chairman says.

'Neither Miss Mykonola nor Mrs Richardson testify in person,' the chairman continues. 'Mr Hobson starts by giving the impression that they think Mr Singh's personality and working style is such that it gives rise to personal difficulties within the team. Under cross-examination, he clarifies this impression is not the one intended to be conveyed. He clarifies it is not the impression he himself is conveying. The suggestion that the team members do not get on, or do not work with each other satisfactorily in the colloquial sense, is not at all being made. What is intended, as understood from his amplifications on the matter, is that there is scope for considerable professional disagreement in the field of work the Controllers engage in, if not dispute, then, at least, discussion and argument as to what is appropriate in terms of managing risks and ensuring appropriate standards. There was a degree of professional disagreement within the team during the course of Mr Singh's employment. The disagreement was entirely at appropriate levels. At no point, prior to selecting Mr Singh for dismissal, does Mr Hobson ever suggest the disagreement is at, or even near, an inappropriate level, on Mr Singh's part, or anyone else's'.

'Mr Hobson accepts that nobody, including Miss Mykonola and Mrs Richardson, ever complained to him that the degree of disagreement was ever at an inappropriate level,' the chairman continues. 'He himself never needed to intervene and take steps to manage the level of disagreement. His testimony on behalf of Miss Mykonola and Mrs Richardson gives a different impression of Mr Singh, one that Miss Mykonola and Mrs Richardson are not trying to suggest. If they are trying to suggest the impression he gives, then the tribunal rejects it in the light of his subsequent amplifications'.

'Moving on to the matter of the relationship between Mr Hobson and Mr Singh,' the chairman continues. 'The tribunal raised the relationship as a matter for question during the discrimination liability hearing. It took the relationship into account in deliberating and deciding on liability. It also considered the relationship when making the orders for reinstatement. The tribunal regards the relationship to be a factor that is highly relevant in the possibility of complying with the reinstatement orders'.

'The respondents' counsel says Mr Hobson cannot countenance Mr Singh's reinstatement because Mr Singh litigated against him,' the chairman continues. 'Mr Hobson never says anything to that effect directly himself. The tribunal does not regard the statement, advanced by the respondents' counsel on his behalf, to reflect his actual view. If such a view resides at the heart of any resistance to reinstatement, then the tribunal does not countenance it because it is rooted in unlawful victimisation on the grounds of race'.

'Turning now to the respondents' submission that Mr Singh does not accept Mr Hobson as his manager,' the chairman continues. 'There is a degree of professional disagreement between Mr Singh and Mr Hobson regarding the issue of whether, for the purpose of operational efficiency, the Controllers should report directly into Mr Ong, the Director of the department, instead of into Mr Hobson. The topic is visited over a period of time during Mr Singh's employment. Mr Hobson even dwells on it when selecting Mr Singh for dismissal. The tribunal rejects the submission that Mr Singh does not accept Mr Hobson's authority because never, prior to the matter of reinstatement coming into play, does Mr Hobson suggest there are any personal difficulties between Mr Singh and any other member of the team, including himself. The tribunal also rejects the submission because Mr Singh's willingness to be reinstated under Mr Hobson, and to serve him faithfully, even after all that he has been subjected to, is sincere, which it could not be if there were any personal difficulties'.

'Taking all of the matters into account,' the chairman continues, 'the respondents come *a long way short* of being able to say compliance with the reinstatement orders is impossible. The tribunal finds the respondents fail to comply with the orders. The tribunal's decision is unanimous. Consequently, the respondents are liable to the payment of an *Additional Award* under the legal remedy of compensation, to which the hearing must now proceed'.

4

INCOMPLETE PROCESS

'Compensation isn't a *punishment* on the respondents,' my counsel explains to me while we wait in the claimants' waiting room for the remedy hearing to reconvene. 'It's a *remedy* for you. Its purpose isn't to *penalise* the respondents for their unlawful conduct. It's to *compensate* you for the damages you sustain; to put you back in the financial position you'd be in if you weren't dismissed wrongfully'.

'I see,' I reply.

'It does this,' she continues, 'by indemnifying you financially for the loss you sustain as a result of the unlawful conduct you suffered. The amount of compensation can't be in excess of the damages you sustain, because any excess would be tantamount to a *penalty* on the respondents and a *profit* for you. The law doesn't permit either of those things'.

'That means the best possible position I can hope to achieve,' I say, 'is where I'm out of pocket only by the expenses I've incurred in seeking justice'.

'Yes,' she replies. 'Your expenses aren't recoverable. You'll always be out of pocket by them'.

'That's so unfair,' I moan. 'They're already huge and will only continue to escalate'.

'That's the law,' she says. 'It's kind of fair, in the sense that it applies both ways. Had you lost your case, then you wouldn't have to reimburse the respondents the expenses they incurred'.

'Hmm, it seems fair in theory,' I reply. 'But, it's mostly unfair in reality. Usually, it's us employees who are the financially struggling party and can't afford to bear even our own costs. Having to bear them is prohibitive to being able to even contemplate standing up for ourselves, let alone actually try it. In practice, the law's biased in favour of the employers. They can do wrongs with confidence in the belief that there's little chance they'll be brought to account'.

'Yes,' she says.

'What it means for me,' I continue, 'is that I can't even achieve breakeven. I'm not looking to profit. I'll be happy with reinstatement. There's no profit in reinstatement. The law means I'll always remain at a loss. That's unfair'.

'The law delivers *legal justice*,' she says. 'Legal justice can sometimes be unfair'.

'Hmm,' I sigh.

'By forcing remedy to compensation,' she continues, 'the respondents bring into play a legal duty on you to mitigate your loss'.

'What do you mean?' I ask.

'Suffering a *wrongdoing*, and the *damage* ensuing from the wrongdoing, are two separate matters,' she says. 'The tribunal established that you suffered wrongdoings. Now, it must establish and quantify the financial damages you suffer consequent to the wrongdoings'.

'Yes,' I agree.

'Your duty to mitigate your loss requires you to take reasonable, proactive steps to avoid suffering any damages,' she says. 'That means finding another job as quickly as possible to replace the loss of income from the one you're dismissed from'.

'Yes, that makes sense,' I say.

'Just because you suffer wrongdoings,' she continues, 'it doesn't automatically follow that you should suffer damage. You could've started a new job the very next day after your notice of termination period ended, and not suffered any loss of income at all'.

'I tried to do that,' I reply, 'but it takes time to get another job'.

'Yes,' she says, 'and tribunals recognise that it can take

time to get another job. They accept there may be some gap in employment. They expect the length of the gap to be reasonable though, maybe a few weeks or a couple of months at most. You've been unemployed since April now. That's nine months. Anything more than a few months starts to raise questions, like, whether *you're* the problem, rather than the job market? Perhaps, you're just not making the expected effort. Perhaps, you're just sitting back and letting your loss accumulate because you think you'll be compensated for it in full'.

'Each profession and industry is different,' I reply. 'In some professions, you can get another job in just an afternoon. In others, it can take months, maybe even years'.

'The average compensation awarded by tribunals is only about nine thousand pounds,' she says. 'The tribunal is going to find itself hard pressed to deviate far north of that, even with your investment banking salary'.

'That's one reason I wanted reinstatement,' I say, 'to avoid this situation and all the uncertainty it entails'.

'We are where we are,' she says as a matter of fact. 'To discharge your duty successfully, you're expected to act like a reasonable person would. The critical word is, *reasonable*. You need only to take reasonable steps. You don't need to take extreme steps, like, uproot yourself from here to take up a job opportunity on the other side of the world'.

'So, if I sustain a loss that could've been avoided by the taking of some reasonable steps, but isn't avoided because I didn't take those steps, then the tribunal won't compensate me for that loss, even though I incurred it,' I say.

'Correct,' she replies. 'For example, if the tribunal thinks you should quite reasonably have managed to get another job within a month, even though you haven't actually found one yet in nine months, it'll cut your loss at one month's worth of income. Your failure to pre-empt damage that's avoidable by the taking of reasonable steps is neglect on your part of your duty to mitigate your loss. The tribunal won't permit you to benefit from your negligence. It won't compensate you where you effectively sat back and allowed your loss to accumulate'.

'So,' I reply, 'I need to reduce my loss as much as I can, and, thereby, reduce the level of compensation that may be awarded'.

'Correct,' she says. 'If you mitigate some loss successfully, then the respondents benefit from your success. Your loss reduces, which, in turn, reduces their exposure to compensation, accordingly'.

'They always seem to have the upper hand,' I moan.

'Your legal duty to mitigate your loss does give them an advantage over you in two ways,' she says. 'It acts for them as a *shield*, allowing them to protect themselves against any unreasonable and negligent conduct on your part. It also acts as a *sword*, allowing them to cut down your loss, even right down to zero, by proving you failed to discharge your duty properly'.

'What about all the mental distress they've put me through?' I ask. 'People get awarded millions for that'.

'Not in this country,' she says. 'Here, it's called *Injury to Feelings*, and the maximum allowed is twenty-five thousand pounds. You really have to have suffered immensely to get anywhere near the maximum amount, like, have been left blind because it was your employers fault you fell into a vat of some toxic chemicals at work. In your case, you'll get a few thousand pounds only'.

'Really? Is that all?' I reply.

'Yes,' she confirms. 'It's across the pond, in America, where your loss might be just one day's earnings, but you can get awarded millions for the mental distress you experienced. Or, your loss might be just the cost of your nice white shirt that a waiter spills a glass of red wine on, but you can get awarded millions for the mental trauma it causes you'.

'I see,' I say.

'That's why they have a litigious culture over there,' she adds. 'People there are on the look out for litigation opportunities to exploit for the mental distress element. We don't have such a culture here because the duty to mitigate loss, and the small Injury to Feelings payments, often mean litigation isn't worth the bother'.

'This doesn't bode well for me,' I say letting out a sigh. 'Plus, we don't have much hearing time left. How are we going to get through a whole hearing on compensation in just the couple of hours of hearing time we have remaining in this session? We only had one day of tribunal time allocated to us'.

~ Wednesday 3rd January 2007, 3:00 p.m. ~

'Mr Singh, is that your signature on the witness statement and is that the evidence you wish to give?' my counsel asks me immediately after I finish swearing to tell the truth at the witness desk.

I have presented the tribunal my statement on my duty to mitigate my loss. It says the following:

> I started searching for another job a year ago, immediately after being told I am selected for dismissal. I had worked in the investment banking sector for twelve years by then, the last nine of those years being specifically in the field of market risk. I started by searching for jobs in risk control and related fields, to which I might be able to transfer my skills and experiences.
>
> My personal experience and knowledge of how the investment banking sector operates informed me that vacancies suitable for me tend to get filled through personal contacts and recruitment agents operating in the sector. I informed my network of relevant personal contacts that I am looking for a

job. I registered myself with three recruitment agencies with whom I believe I could achieve a good coverage of the vacancies available on the job market.

My experience also informed me that job opportunities suitable for a candidate as experienced and specialised as I am are scarce on the open job market due to a number of factors. First, the pyramidal organisational structure in companies means there are fewer positions as you go up the organisation. Second, incumbents tend not to vacate senior roles as frequently as junior roles. Third, employers tend not to create fresh senior positions as frequently as they do junior ones. Fourth, employers prefer to fill senior vacancies by promoting internal candidates from within the organisation, rather than by recruiting candidates from the external job market. The scarcity of suitable job opportunities on the open job market makes finding another job quite a difficult task for me.

To improve my chances of getting back into work, I also applied for some vacancies calling for less experience than I possess. But, employers simply do not proceed with my applications for such jobs because my profile does not match their requirements.

Despite all of my efforts, I have not managed to secure another job yet. Based on my experience, I expect considerable time could pass before I manage to gain employment again. Katia Mykonola, being my peer and obvious comparator, when made redundant from her previous employment, spent eighteen months searching for a job before finally finding employment at the bank as my colleague.

Immediately after being informed I am selected

for dismissal, I contacted Paul Blessed. He recruited me into my Market Risk Controller job at the respondent bank, and was my first manager there. He subsequently left the bank, but we remain in touch. He now works as the Director of Risk Management at JBC, a Japanese financial institution. I told him I am being dismissed and I urgently need another job. I asked him to let me know if he has any vacancies that might be suitable for me, or if he becomes aware of any. He said he did not know of any at the time, but would keep an eye out and let me know if he hears of any anywhere.

On 15th February, Danny No, a close friend of mine who works at UBE, a European financial institution, registered my details with its Human Resources department for any vacancies that might arise in its Market Risk department. I know Danny from my previous employment of six years at UBE. On 7th September, I applied for the Risk Analyst vacancy at UBE through him. My application was rejected because I am too senior for the role.

I have been considered for eleven specific jobs, but only three of them are commensurate with my level of seniority and experience.

One of those three jobs is the Head of Derivative Products Risk vacancy in the Market Risk Department of the respondent bank itself. I applied for it on 27th January, after being informed I am being dismissed and while I was still under my notice of termination. The role heads up a team in the Market Risk Department. It reports directly into Simon Ong. It is equal in rank and seniority to Neil's role. The role requirements and my profile are a good match. A panel of three people interviewed me for the role. But, the bank filled the vacancy by promoting a person from within the team under the role, who was already performing the role in an acting capacity.

Another of those three jobs is the vacancy that heads up a risk team in the Market Risk department of CEFP, another European financial institution. I applied for it on 18th January through the recruitment agency representing the employer. CEFP eventually gave the role to an internal candidate.

The last of those three jobs is the Operations Manager vacancy at Tick-It, an institution that provides a market data service to financial institutions. The role is not in the field of risk. I applied for it on 30th August through the recruitment agency representing the employer. Tick-It interviewed me on 5th September. It subsequently rejected me saying my technical skills and experience are in excess of its requirements. The role requirements and my profile did not match well.

The other eight jobs are too junior for me. The role requirements and my profile do not match up well. I am not at all surprised the employers rejected me for each and every one of them.

From October onwards, there were not any suitable vacancies on the job market for me to apply for. Seasonal factors tend to render the later part of the year extremely quiet in relation to recruitment of senior and experienced candidates. One factor contributing to this is that by then, incumbents in senior positions have accrued ten months of their annual performance related bonuses, which they would forgo if they resign before banking. They tend to remain in their positions into the forthcoming trading year, until after they have safely banked their bonuses. This factor is so significant that it causes opportunities suitable for me to dry up in the later months of the year. Employers cannot justify the considerable expense entailed in compensating new joiners with *Golden Hello* payments for any bonuses they forgo by jumping ship, when they can avoid the expense altogether simply by waiting a few months until the individuals have banked their bonuses. Furthermore, employers tend to have spent the vast majority of their annual budgets by the end of October, meaning they cannot afford to make large golden hello payments, anyway.

'Yes,' I answer firmly.

My counsel gives way to the respondents counsel to cross-examine me.

'On losing your job at the bank, there is no reason why you should experience difficulty in getting another similar job in the financial sector,' the respondents' counsel says.

'There is,' I reply. 'The bank's policy on giving references to prospective employers is to communicate the individual's final appraisal score and the line manager's comments. My final appraisal includes manager's comments to the effect that I *need to take greater account of the regulator's requirements and embrace change more positively*. Those comments will be communicated to employers seeking a reference on me. No right-minded employer can hire me after receiving a reference saying that. The risk is too great for them to take'.

'In your attempt to find another job, you make use of only two personal acquaintances,' she says.

'I made use of all acquaintances who I thought might be useful,' I reply. 'I have documentary evidence relating only to two, though, because communication with most acquaintances occurred orally, in an informal way, without any documents evidencing it'.

'The evidence you provide is all the evidence that you

are entitled to rely on,' she asserts. 'The evidence shows you make use of two personal acquaintances only. Although you contact Paul Blessed, the Director of Risk Management at the Japanese financial institution, in January, you never contact him again. He has no way of knowing you are still searching for a job'.

'Whether or not I contact him again,' I reply, 'is irrelevant because I know if he has any news for me about a possible job opportunity, then he'll contact me, regardless, even if he thinks I'm employed somewhere. However, contrary to your claim, the documentary evidence on page 635 of the evidence bundles shows I contacted him again about job opportunities, in March'.

Turning to page 635 in the evidence bundles and addressing the respondents' counsel, the chairman interjects, 'what do you make of the evidence Mr Singh refers to?'

'Er,' she mumbles reviewing the document. 'Hmm, it proves his point,' she concedes in disappointed tone.

Addressing me, the chairman asks, 'how big is the Japanese institution and its Risk department?'

'It's an international bank,' I answer. 'Its Risk department in London is about the same size as the respondents' Market Risk Department. I don't know accurately the overall size of the institution, but I know it's large and long established'.

The chairman signals the respondents' counsel to continue.

'Regarding your testimony in relation to Danny No,' she resumes, 'the close friend you refer to who is an employee at UBE. Other than speaking with him on the 15th of February and the 7th of September, you make no other contact with him to try to find a job through him'.

'To the contrary,' I reply, 'I have regular and frequent contact with him because we run together on Saturday mornings in Regent's Park'.

The chairman interjects,' Mr Singh, for how long have

you been running together?'

'We started in the summer of 2002,' I answer. 'So, four and a half years now'.

'Do you run every Saturday?' the chairman asks.

'We run most Saturday mornings,' I answer. 'We don't run, if it's raining; we're not diehards. We'll miss some weekends because of other commitments, like, being away on holiday. And, we stopped for several months after I broke my leg'.

The chairman signals the respondents' counsel to continue.

'While running together,' she resumes, 'you do not speak to him about job opportunities'.

'I do,' I reply. 'Being dismissed from my job and being unemployed are landmark events in my life. Your suggestion that my close friend and I don't dwell on such significant personal experiences is unrealistic to the ridiculous. Conversations with my friends and relatives very quickly gravitate to my dismissal and lack of employment situation. Besides, the documentary evidence on pages 273 and 528 of the evidence bundles shows I spoke to him specifically about job opportunities on at least two further occasions'.

Turning to the referenced pages and addressing the respondents' counsel, the chairman interjects, 'what do you make of the documents Mr Singh refers to?'

'Er, they prove he discussed job opportunities with Mr No on those two occasions also,' she concedes in annoyed tone.

The chairman signals her to continue.

'You say you apply for a job at Leibermann Brothers, an American financial institution,' she says. 'The documentary evidence you provide shows only that you send your CV to the institution, not that you apply for any job there'.

'Why else would I send my CV to them?' I reply. 'I applied for the job orally, during a phone conversation with the recruitment agent representing them. I don't have any documentary evidence of the phone call; it was oral. The agent asked me to email my CV to him, which I did following the phone call'.

'There is no documentary evidence showing you apply for the job,' she says. 'In fact, you do not apply for the job'.

'I did apply for it,' I assert. 'I applied orally over the phone'.

'Actually, you did not,' she repeats.

'I did,' I repeat.

'I put it to you, Mr Singh, you did not,' she asserts in harsh tone.

Addressing her sternly, the chairman interjects, 'I warned you about this before, during the liability hearing! You cannot make a positive case out of putting the same negative construct to him again, and again, when he has already answered clearly and consistently! If you have evidence that is contrary to his answer, then disclose it! Otherwise, move on!'

'With respect, Sir,' she says in subservient tone, 'the documentary evidence he provides does not prove he applies for the job'.

'It also does not prove your case, that he did not apply for it,' the chairman asserts. 'Move on!'

'Moving on, then,' she resumes. 'You say you apply for a job at LBOS, a UK financial institution. There is absolutely no documentary evidence relating to that job. In fact, you do not apply for any such job'.

'That's incorrect,' I reply. 'I applied for it, and the evidence is in the bundles presented to the tribunal'.

'Would you care to tell the tribunal which page number it may find the evidence on,' she says in confident tone.

'Sure, just give me a minute to search through the bundles,' I say reaching for the bundles of evidence available to me at the witness stand.

Addressing the chairman, my counsel interjects, 'Sir, I

have looked through the bundles thoroughly. I could not find any documentary evidence in them relating to that job'.

Turning my head to my right to face her, I say, 'oh, that's worrying. It *has* to be there, though'.

'Let us move on then,' the chairman interjects, 'rather than waste time searching for something that is not there'.

'I've found it,' I say. 'It's on page 927. The print is rather feint and is in quite a small font size, but you should just about be able to make out what it says'.

Turning to the page and addressing the respondents' counsel, the chairman asks, 'what do you make of the evidence?'

'Er, hmm, it shows he applies for the job,' she concedes in disappointed tone.

Addressing my counsel with a smile, the chairman says, 'you really must learn to trust your clients more'.

'Yes, Sir,' she replies with a return smile.

The chairman signals the respondents' counsel to continue.

'Moving on,' she says. 'You do not make use of any Internet websites in your job search. If you were genuinely looking for a job, then you would use Internet websites'.

'I didn't register on any websites because recruitment agents are the appropriate channels for finding employment in my specific circumstances,' I reply. 'I'm confident that the agents I'm registered with provide me with a good coverage of the vacancies and opportunities available on the job market'.

'You do not use the website, *eFinanceJobs*, that Mr Hobson refers you to,' she says. 'You do not apply for any of the sixty or so jobs he prints off the adverts for from the website and sends you by post'.

Addressing the respondents' counsel, the chairman interjects, 'is your point that he fails to mitigate his loss because he does not make use of the website, or because he does not apply for any of the jobs Mr Hobson forwards to him'.

'The latter, Sir,' she clarifies.

The chairman signals me to answer.

'I didn't use the eFinanceJobs website that Neil references,' I reply. 'I can't tell simply from looking at the information shown on the adverts he sent me whether or not I applied for the jobs underlying them. Virtually all of the adverts are placed by recruitment agents, rather than by the employers behind them. That's clearly visible because the adverts show the agents' identities, but not the employers'. I may very well have applied, or have been considered, for many of the jobs through my agents, not least because they're responsible for placing a significant portion of the adverts Neil sent. Neil merely forwarded adverts to me, without saying anything. He didn't say what I should do with them. He didn't say I should apply for them. Nevertheless, I took the initiative to review the adverts he sent me for appropriateness and relevance to my profile. I found the vast majority are inappropriate and irrelevant because they're in fields and disciplines in which I don't have any experience. He's trying to give the impression the job market is buoyant with vacancies that are suitable for me, by mindlessly printing off as many job adverts as he can find. He's not given the slightest thought and consideration to their appropriateness and relevance to me, specifically. His priority is *quantity*, not *relevance*. Many of the adverts are duplicates, triplicates, and even quadruplicates. That's how mindlessly he's approached this. He didn't even bother to check if he's sending me unique adverts. The number of vacancies, sixty you say, is significantly inflated because of the duplication. His concern is *appearance*, not *substance*'.

'You do nothing at all to ascertain whether or not you applied for the vacancies that are relevant to your profile,' she says.

'That's incorrect,' I reply. 'I extracted the adverts that looked as though they might be relevant to me in some way, and I assessed them. I concluded my agents had covered them all. I came across one advert that is placed by one of my agents, but which I couldn't recall the agency ever bringing to my attention. So, I took that one up with the agent. He told me that they had screened me out because I was too senior for it. He didn't consider it necessary to take the further step of bringing the vacancy and his decision to my attention. This is shown by the email correspondence about this between the agent and myself, on page 647 in the bundles of evidence. I find the agent's explanation entirely consistent with my understanding of how they operate. They don't waste their time dwelling on negatives; they focus their energies on positives and on moving forwards'.

'Many of the adverts originate from recruitment agents with whom you are not registered,' she says. 'You do nothing at all to register yourself with them and apply for those jobs. You should have registered with them. You simply are not proactive enough in searching for a job'.

'The agents I'm registered with covered those jobs too,' I reply. 'I didn't register with more agents because I'm confident the three I'm with give me a good coverage of the vacancies available on the job market'.

The chairman interjects, 'Mr Singh, do you not think you ought to register with more recruitment agents, given the three you are with manage to generate only two opportunities in eight months that are commensurate with your profile?'

'No,' I answer, 'because it's not due to any lack of effort on their part in trying to find job opportunities for me. It's simply due to the scarcity of vacancies on the job market that are commensurate with my profile'.

'Is the scarcity not all the more reason to register with more agents?' the chairman asks.

'No,' I answer. 'I'm confident the three I'm with provide a good coverage. I don't believe registering with more would increase my exposure'.

'Did you contemplate a more radical job search, that is, outside of the field of risk?' the chairman asks.

'I looked for jobs outside of the field of risk, but not outside of the financial services sector,' I answer.

'Do you think you ought to consider a much more radical job search and, perhaps, contemplate other sectors besides finance?' the chairman asks.

'Only nine months have passed since my dismissal,' I answer. 'I think looking outside the financial sector so soon is a bit premature. It took Katia one and a half years to find a job. Also, employers aren't likely to take me seriously for roles that are radically different from the ones my skills and experiences relate to. For example, even though I'm a qualified Chartered Accountant, an accountancy practice is highly unlikely to hire me because I've been out of the profession for thirteen years now'.

The chairman signals the respondents' counsel to continue.

'Quantify how much personal time you spent each month on searching and applying for jobs,' she resumes.

'Er, it's difficult to say,' I reply.

'Do not evade the question, Mr Singh,' she says aggressively. 'Answer it properly!'

'Initially, I spent a considerable amount of time preparing my CV, letting my contacts know I'm looking for work, meeting up with recruitment agents, explaining my situation and needs to them, and registering with them,' I answer. 'Then, on an on-going basis, I spent time liaising and working with agents as and when job opportunities arose'.

'So, Mr Singh,' she says, 'from your rather vague answer, it is clear all you do is: register with three agents; occasionally discuss jobs with them; and contact some personal acquaintances. Clearly, you are not at all proactive in looking for another job. You do not devote much of your personal time to the task. You do not apply to employers directly yourself. You should have applied to employers directly too'.

'Registering with agents, working with them, and utilising my personal contacts *are* proactive initiatives on my part,' I assert. 'Recruitment agents represent the main route into another job in my circumstances and profession. They're effectively *gatekeepers* to the jobs that are suitable for me. Employers reach out into the job market via recruitment agents. I'm certain my agents work very hard on trying to find me a job because they stand to earn a commission of around thirty to forty per cent of my total compensation from the employer they manage to place me with. Having said that, whenever it was possible, which is rarely, I applied directly to employers too. I managed to find some vacancies by browsing some employers' websites. I have provided the tribunal documentary evidence showing that I also applied directly to some employers'.

'There are a number of vacancies Neil sends you, which you do not apply for,' she says disapprovingly.

'Stop!' the chairman interjects sternly addressing her. 'The *respondents* are the wrongdoers here, not Mr Singh! As the wrongdoers' representative, you ought not to be so eager to criticise his attempts at mitigating the damage they cause him!'

'But, Sir,' she replies in respectful tone, 'there are jobs he does not apply for'.

'It is impossible in practice for him to look at every single job opportunity available on the job market,' the chairman rebuts. 'There has to be an acceptance that it is impossible for any reasonable person to be exhaustive, and that he will miss *many* opportunities. Registering with every single recruitment agent is equally impossible and, perhaps, even undesirable because it might give the impression he is desperate. The duty upon him is to act *reasonably*, not perfectly and exhaustively! Explain to the tribunal why you think the steps he took are not entirely reasonable?'

'Because he is not proactive in his job search,' she answers.

'He seems to be sufficiently proactive,' the chairman rebuts. 'He instructs and works with recruitment agents in a reasonable manner. If there is another good source of jobs he is reasonably expected to utilise, but he does not, then he might be negligent in his duty to mitigate his loss'.

'The eFinanceJobs website is a good source,' she replies. 'He does not use it'.

'It does not appear to be a mandatory source,' the chairman rebuts. 'It is dominated by recruitment agents; he is registered with agents already'.

'The website shows the job market is buoyant with vacancies,' she replies. 'His job search is inadequate because he does not pursue, personally himself, the opportunities shown on it'.

'Why,' the chairman asks, 'does his answer, *the agents pursued the opportunities on my behalf*, not suggest an entirely adequate job search?'

'Er,' she mumbles.

'If he did not engage any agents at all,' the chairman continues, 'then he might be inadequate in his duty. Mr Hobson's act of forwarding job adverts to him does not heighten his duty in any way, nor does it prove any failure on his part. Move on!'

'Moving on,' she says. 'The job adverts show the job market is buoyant with job opportunities in the field of risk,' she resumes.

'Some of the adverts relate to the field of risk,' I reply. 'Apart from the odd one or two that might be somewhat suited to my profile, the rest all relate to junior profiles. What the adverts actually show is that the job market is buoyant for junior candidates, not for candidates as experienced as I am'.

'I have no further questions,' she says giving way to my counsel to re-examine me.

'Upon being dismissed, in addition to devoting time to

looking for another job, what else did you devote time to?' my counsel asks.

'I spent a massive portion of my time trying to address the respondents' unlawful and racially motivated conduct against me,' I answer. 'Preparing for the so-called *consultation* meetings took up a huge portion of my time. Drafting and finalising the numerous formal grievances and appeals I lodged, preparing the evidence for them, attending the hearing meetings, and participating in resolving the issues, were very laborious and hugely time-consuming tasks. They spanned over a period of eight months. Also, complying with the legal procedures and preparing for the tribunal hearing are mammoth undertakings. They consumed huge amounts of my time over a period of five months. They demanded so much time that I often worked on them all day and also into the nights and the early hours of the mornings'.

'Can you describe how you felt about being dismissed from work?' she asks.

'The false negative remarks about my performance that Neil recorded officially in my final appraisal cause me a lot of mental distress,' I answer. 'The remarks signify serious ineptitude on my part. Never before have I been criticised thus by him or anyone else. The bank's policy says performance issues are supposed to be monitored on an on-going basis, so timely corrective action can be taken and so there will be no surprises in appraisals. However, Neil's criticisms came suddenly and from out of nowhere. Furthermore, they stretch back years beyond the period that was being appraised. They are not only blatantly false, but also completely contrary to all of my previous performance appraisals, which are all good. The false criticisms are a huge source of embarrassment and distress for me because I had worked as a Market Risk Controller for nine years by then and should not be so inept as Neil records that I am. It defies belief that I could have reached a senior professional status and still be so inept.

One by one, each and every officer of the bank, who was responsible for investigating the issues, endorsed his remarks about me. Rather than call him out, and call the discrimination out, they all backed him up completely and perpetuated the embarrassment and anguish I feel. Not one of them demonstrated the personal integrity needed to ensure the effectiveness of the grievance procedures. They all turned out to be the respondents' *yes-men*. Their endorsements of his conduct and their *towing the party line* fuelled the anguish I feel. The criticisms Neil makes of me not only deny me my good performance level for that year, but also seriously threaten my career prospects. Just take a look at how they've impacted me already. They fed into the redundancy selection exercise and cost me my job and career at the bank. They fed into the bonus-setting process and deprived me of thousands of pounds of income. They harm me in very real and significant ways. I fear they will also feed into references the bank provides to prospective employers for future employments. The bank's policy on references, which is supplied to the tribunal in the bundles of evidence, is to disclose the details of the last official performance appraisal, that is, the performance rating score and the *manager's comments*. When viewed in the cold light of day, the negative remarks will preclude employers from hiring me. The effects of the criticisms are to render me unemployable. They destroy my career. All of this is a constant source of great mental anguish for me. It constantly undermines my peace of mind, keeping me from falling asleep every night and waking me up in the mornings'.

~ Wednesday 3rd January 2007, 4:00 p.m. ~

'I do solemnly, sincerely and truly declare and affirm that the evidence I shall give shall be the truth the whole truth and nothing but the truth,' Neil swears in at the witness desk.

I sit in my usual spot in the public gallery, immediately behind my counsel and her assistant, with a clear side on view of Neil. He has presented the tribunal his statement on my duty to mitigate my loss. It says the following:

> In my experience, the job market in the field of market risk is extremely buoyant. I am very surprised Ranjit Singh has not yet found another job.
>
> Throughout the period of litigation, I identified job vacancies on the job market that I think are suitable for him. I did this because I was aware, through my legal advisors, that he has not found another job yet. I simply entered the keywords, *market risk jobs*, into an Internet search engine. The search returned a lot of results. Then, I simply looked into the very first result in the list, which happened to be the *eFinanceJobs* website. I found many job opportunities on it. I did not have to look particularly hard, or even long, to find such a large number of vacancies. I looked on this one website only, rather than at all of the results the search returned. The sheer number of job vacancies I was able to find with such ease clearly proves the market for market risk jobs is very buoyant.
>
> From time to time, between August and November, I printed off job adverts that I found on the website and sent them to Ranjit. I have a good understanding and appreciation of his skills and capabilities. I believe all of the jobs I forwarded to him are suitable for him. Even though many are clearly more junior than his Market Risk Controller role at the bank, I believe they are suitable for him. He should have applied for every single one of them. He has the skills and

experience to perform them all. I expected him to apply for them all, and to have gotten a job by now.

I am genuinely surprised he has not yet found another job because, in my experience, the job market for Market Risk Controllers, Risk Analysts, Risk Reporters, and Risk Managers has been very buoyant throughout 2006. The large number of vacancies I found with such little effort proves this to be the case. Given his skills and experience, I expected him to find another job within two months of his dismissal. I appreciate there would be a series of interviews that could take some time to set up and go through, but I think two months is a wholly realistic and generous timeframe. I am utterly dumbfounded that he still has not found a job in nine months.

Regarding references for employment the bank will give to prospective employers, the only information that will feed into them is: the description of his Market Risk Controller role at the bank; the commencement date of his employment; his dismissal date; and the rating scores of his last two year-end performance appraisals. The *Manager's Comments* section of the appraisals and the manager's remarks contained in them is not disclosed to prospective employers. When prospective employers approach me with requests for informal, oral references, I refuse them; I refer them to the bank's HR department for formal, written references.

'Mr Hobson, is that your signature on the witness statement and is that the evidence you wish to give?' the respondents' counsel asks.

'Yes,' he replies.

She gives way to my counsel to cross-examine him.

'Do you accept that virtually none of the job adverts you forward to Ranjit disclose the identities of the employers underlying them?' my counsel asks.

'Yes,' he answers.

'Do you accept that many adverts are duplicates, triplicates, and even quadruplicates?' she asks.

'Er, yes,' he confirms.

The chairman interjects, 'Mr Hobson, do you accept that recruitment agents placed virtually all of the job adverts you reference?'

'Yes,' he accepts.

'Do you accept agents represent the main route to employments in the sorts of roles you identify?' the chairman asks.

'Er,' he stalls. 'I wouldn't rely on recruitment agents only. I'd consider every possible avenue'.

The chairman signals my counsel to continue.

'The impression the adverts give is the job market is buoyant only in junior level vacancies, which call for up to five years of experience,' she says. 'Ranjit has nine years of experience in market risk, and twelve years in investment banking, overall'.

'Although none of the adverts call for nine years of experience,' he replies, 'some call for *five-plus* years. That's enough to indicate a senior level role'.

'None of them call for *nine to ten* years of experience,' she says.

'Perhaps not,' he replies. 'There are some for five-plus years, though'.

'The absence of vacancies calling for nine to ten years of experience indicates the market for jobs requiring nine to ten years of experience is not buoyant,' she says.

'No, their absence doesn't indicate that,' he asserts.

'Moving on,' she says. 'When Ranjit seeks reinstatement at the bank in the Market Risk Associate vacancy, Mr Ong argues that his reinstatement into the role is impossible because: he is too senior for it; and he will report into the retained Controller, who is his peer and with whom his level of seniority clashes. Mr Ong says these factors will imbalance the workplace environment and lead to issues, which will cause disruptions. If Ranjit, with his twelve years of experience, applies for a vacancy that requires up to five years of experience only, then would that not cause similar problems for the prospective employer? Problems, such as, his level of seniority clashing with his prospective manager's, and his profile being out of kilter with his prospective colleagues?'

'Er, no, it wouldn't,' he asserts.

'Why not?' she asks.

'Er,' he stalls. 'Hmm,' he muses. 'Because his twelve years of experience is *technical* experience only, not *management* experience also'.

'Turning to the performance appraisal rating scores that you say the bank will disclose in references for employments to prospective employers,' she says. Ranjit's final assessment score, of 4/8 for 2005, will impact negatively on his chance of finding another job'.

'His score of 6/8 for the previous year will also be disclosed in references,' he replies.

'The latest score of 4/8 is lower than the earlier score of 6/8,' she says.

'Yes,' he replies.

'His final score of 4/8 means his chance of finding another job is lower than it would be if he had achieved a score of 5/8, or 6/8,' she says.

'Hmm, I'm not sure,' he replies.

The chairman interjects, 'Mr Hobson, we are trying to understand the impact of appraisal scores disclosed in references. Will the lower appraisal score of 4/8 adversely affect Mr Singh's chance of finding another job?'

'Er,' he mumbles. 'Hmm, yes,' he concedes reluctantly.

'I have no further questions,' my counsel says.

Addressing the respondents' counsel, the chairman asks, 'do you wish to re-examine your witness?'

'No, Sir,' she replies.

'Mr Hobson, you are released,' the chairman says. 'You may leave the witness stand'.

Addressing both counsels, the chairman says, 'the tribunal has been presented with documentary and oral evidence regarding Mr Singh's duty to mitigate his loss, and the amount of loss he sustains. There is no time remaining in this hearing session for the tribunal to be presented with submissions of arguments for and against compensation. Without these submissions, the hearing process is incomplete and the tribunal cannot deliberate the amount of financial compensation to award, if any at all. The hearing must be adjourned and reconvened at a future date. The earliest timeslot available for a reconvened session is the 21st to the 24th of August. All parties are to reconvene here then. The tribunal is to be presented with updates on mitigation over the adjournment period, and submissions of arguments on compensation. The hearing is adjourned'.

'All stand,' the courtroom attendant cries out.

5

RANJIT SINGH'S UPDATE TESTIMONY

~ Tuesday 21st August 2007, 10:00 a.m. ~

'Mr Singh, is that your signature on the witness statement and is that the evidence you wish to give?' my counsel asks me immediately after I finish swearing in at the witness desk.

I have presented the tribunal my statement on my duty to mitigate my loss during the eight-month adjournment period of the remedy hearing, along with over a thousand pages of documentary evidence. My statement says the following:

> The respondent bank has been in business for over a hundred years. It has employed countless thousands of people during its long existence. Being a financial services provider, employing people is a major part of its operating activities. It is an experienced expert in the subject of employment. It brands its employment policies with the logo, *"Best bank to work for"*. In its employment policies, it boasts it applies the best employment practices there are, and that it stands out as a, *"best practice employer"*.
>
> The respondents' initial reason for refusing the remedy of reinstatement is because I litigated against them. They stated the reason boldly before the tribunal and the members of the public present at the remedy hearing on 15th December 2006.

The reason evidences that they, a *"best practice employer"*, stigmatise me for litigating against them. Even though they left me no other option, but to litigate, and even though I litigated entirely in good faith and with good cause, still, they stigmatise me for litigating. Only upon being admonished by the tribunal that they cannot rely on the reason, because it is an unlawful basis for refusing reinstatement, do they then supersede it with a lawful reason. Their act, of superseding their initial unlawful reason with an alternative lawful one, is merely a tactic to front their genuine, socially unacceptable reason with a disingenuous, socially acceptable one. Such is the conduct of the, *"best bank to work for"*, and a, *"best practice employer"*. I am sure I receive the same treatment from prospective employers too. Prospective employers also stigmatise and victimise me for litigating against my former employers, as the respondents do. Unlike the respondents, they are discreet. They are not so audacious and tactless as to disclose their genuine, unlawful reason, like the respondents did so blatantly before everyone present in the courtroom. Instead, they exercise discretion, and take care only to proffer alternative lawful reasons that they know they can get away with safely.

Having spent four years in the accountancy profession training and qualifying as a Chartered Accountant, I started working in the investment banking sector in April 1994. A few years into my career in banking, my employer at the time, UBE, an established European financial institution, promoted me to its corporate title of Associate Director. Two years later, I was headhunted by one of its competitors, CEFP, another European financial institution. It offered to double my remuneration package and promote me to the higher corporate title of Vice President. I accepted, and moved. The titles, Associate Director and Vice President, are labels institutions designate to employees and roles in order to convey the level of experience and seniority associated with them. This practice is common at institutions throughout the sector. After six months at CEFP, I left to take a career break and travel a bit. Six months later, I took up employment at the respondent bank in the Market Risk Controller role. I had accumulated twelve years of experience in investment banking by the time the respondents dismissed me. I am perceived in the job market as being equivalent in seniority and experience as Neil Hobson, my line manager.

For the role of Market Risk Controller, the respondent bank requires over six years of relevant experience in market risk. I more than satisfy this requirement, and all of the other requirements for the role. The bank requires over eight years of relevant experience for a Head of Risk position in the department, being the type of position Neil Hobson holds. I satisfy this, and also all of the other requirements for a Head of Risk role. I support my claim with documentary evidence showing that in February 2006, the bank's interview panel confirmed that I am a strong candidate for the Head of Derivative Products Risk vacancy I applied for, even though I did not get the job.

Job opportunities in market risk at my level of seniority rarely appear on the job market due to a number of factors.

One factor is the pyramidal organisational structure of institutions, which means there are drastically fewer senior roles than junior ones.

Even though this factor is axiomatic, I support my testimony with documentary evidence from recruitment agents.

Another factor is employers' preference and common practice to fill senior vacancies from within the organisation by promoting internal candidates, rather than by recruiting candidates from the external job market. I support my testimony with documentary evidence from recruitment agents, and the fact that the respondent bank itself also prefers this common practice. Its policy documents state clearly, *"internal recruitment and internal promotion are our preferred practices"*. I provide documentary evidence showing it acted in accordance with this policy when it recruited people into a number of vacancies in its Market Risk Department over the course of my employment.

Back in December 2003, Simon Ong created a fresh new Head of Market Risk Control role. He filled it by promoting an internal candidate, my colleague at the time, who had been the longest serving Market Risk Controller. The bank advertised the vacancy internally only. It never advertised it externally on the open job market. Promoting the internal candidate resulted in the Controller role he had occupied becoming vacant, which the bank then sought to fill. First, it tried to fill it with an internal candidate. Only after having tried and failed to find any suitable candidates internally, did it then go on to look at candidates on the external job market, from where it eventually filled the vacancy in May 2004 with Katia Mykonola. Then, around October 2004, when the Head of Market Risk Control vacated his position to take up employment at another financial institution, the bank did not look to the external job market for a candidate to replace him. Instead, it enlarged Katia's and my roles to subsume his responsibilities. This is a form of internal promotion of our roles. Then, it created two fresh new roles under us, the Market Risk Associate roles, to whom some of our simpler responsibilities would be reassigned. Again, it firstly sought to fill these freshly created roles with internal candidates. Three internal candidates expressed an interest. Katia and I interviewed them. Two turned out to be unsuitable. We rejected them. The other one was suitable. But, he subsequently withdrew his interest because he decided to take up another internal opportunity instead. Only after trying and failing to fill the vacancies with internal candidates did the bank look to the external job market for candidates, from where it eventually filled the vacancies with Mary Richardson and Anthony Grenfell. All of this shows clearly that internal recruitment is the bank's preferred practice. Other employers do the same.

The common and preferred practice of internal recruitment tends to prevent vacancies that are commensurate with my level of seniority from reaching the external job market. It tends to lead to junior level roles, which become vacant due to internal promotions, and remain unfilled from within the organisation, ending up on the external job market.

Another factor, contributing to vacancies in market risk that are commensurate with my level of seniority being scarce on the open job market, is employers' tendency to impose conditions that discourage incumbents in senior positions from resigning their employments voluntarily. Common employment practices in the sector include the imposition of conditions, such as, long notice periods, and deferred bonus payments. Long notice periods make it harder for employees to move because they make them less attractive to prospective employers. Deferred bonus payments, which incumbents will forfeit if they resign within a specified time period, usually two years from the bonus award date, make resignation an unattractive prospect for incumbents from a personal financial perspective. The respondent bank too practises these two industry common practices. My employment contract with it contains a long three-month notice of resignation period. Correspondences from it regarding my bonus awards show that it subjects my bonuses to two-year deferment periods, the terms of which are that I will forfeit the deferred amounts it is holding on to, if I resign voluntary within the two-year deferment period. The effect of each year's bonus being subjected to a two-year deferment period is to lock me into employment with it for a rolling two-year period, unless I am willing to forfeit my previous two years of earnings it is holding on to.

In my experience, employers exercise great care to recruit only candidates whose profiles match their requirements well. Even though this seems axiomatic, I support it with documentary evidence from recruitment agents, and also by showing the respondent bank does so too. The bank refused to reinstate me into the Market Risk Associate vacancy on the basis that the position is at a level below the Controller role I held, and because it reports into Katia, my peer. The fact that I am capable of performing the role quite comfortably is insufficient for the bank to reinstate me into it. It also refused to reinstate me into a Risk Reporter vacancy on the basis that the role is *different* from the Controller role I performed. Again, the fact that I am capable of performing the role quite easily is insufficient for it to reinstate me into it. During the adjournment period of the remedy hearing, in April 2007, I saw the bank advertise a Market Risk Analyst vacancy on its website. I applied for it. The bank rejected my application saying my skills and experience exceed those required for the role. Again, the fact that I am capable of performing the role quite comfortably is insufficient for it to recruit me into the vacancy.

If the bank did not dismiss me, then I would be looking at positions equivalent to Neil's, in terms of seniority and experience. I am generally screened out for vacancies designated below this level because employers exercise great care to ensure they only recruit individuals whose profiles match their needs well.

The scarcity of vacancies on the job market matching my profile makes my job search extremely difficult. The overwhelming majority of vacancies are too junior for me. It is junior level vacancies that come up time after time. Nevertheless, I tried to get whatever jobs were available, junior ones included. My applications were unsuccessful because my profile exceeds the employers' requirements. I am still willing to be reinstated into a junior vacancy at the respondent bank.

I was exposed to waves of cost cutting and redundancies at my various employers in most years of my career in investment banking, including a couple of times at the respondent bank. I never experienced redundancy before my unfair dismissal. I always managed to survive in my jobs. I attribute my survival to the fact that my performance and contribution are always high, which provides some safeguard in the form of a lower chance of being let go. I believe I am being quite reasonable in thinking my chances of experiencing redundancy during my career are low.

When employers in the financial sector wish to recruit experienced and qualified candidates from the external job market, they rarely advertise the vacancies directly themselves. They tend to use the services of intermediary recruitment agencies that market the roles on their behalves and source suitable candidates from their registers. The respondent bank does this too. It did so during the course of my employment. Back in December 2003, we looked for external candidates for the Market Risk Controller vacancy in my team via the services of nine agencies. Then, in the second half of 2004, we looked for external candidates for the two Associate vacancies in our team via the services of ten agencies. The bank never communicated any of these vacancies to external candidates directly itself. Recruitment agencies are the main sources available to me for finding another job because they are effectively gatekeepers to the relevant employment opportunities on the job market.

Employers typically instruct several agencies simultaneously for any particular vacancy. The respondent bank instructed nine agents when it recruited for the Controller vacancy, and ten in relation to the Associate vacancies. The effect of this common practice of instructing multiple agents is that vacancies reach a wide target audience of external candidates by the market coverage provided by each individual agency. The practice also means I need only register myself with a handful of agencies in order to gain exposure to most of the available vacancies.

Prior to the discrimination liability hearing in December 2006, I was registered with three recruitment agencies. I believe three are sufficient to achieve a good coverage of the jobs available on the external job market. During the remedy hearing in January 2007, the respondents criticised me severely for using only three agencies in my job search. They complained that I should have used more, if I were serious about finding a job. I do not believe registering with more agents increases my exposure to the available opportunities. Nevertheless, in order to address their criticisms, and only in order to address their criticisms, I registered myself with twenty-three more agents during the adjournment period of the remedy hearing. The only effect this had is that I am approached by lots of agents for the exact same job opportunities that my original three agents approach me for. I provide the tribunal documentary evidence supporting my testimony.

Recruitment agents represent my main route back into employment. I have a heavy reliance on them. This means I need to ensure I keep them on my side. I need to cooperate with them and allow them to participate in decisions about my job search, so they may expedite earning their commission by placing me in a job as quickly as possible. I need to react positively to their ideas and proposals about my career, and go along with their advice, decisions, and wishes. I need to make sure I perform well when they progress my applications to interviews with their clients, the employers. I must not do anything that might undermine or sabotage their investment of effort in me to earn fees and commissions. My dependency on them means my job search is not in my hands only; it is in theirs too. Their involvement injects a level of independence and external control, which has the positive effect of ensuring I do not scupper any opportunities purposely, because any negative behaviour on my part runs the risk of alienating them and cutting off my main source of employment opportunities. The independence and control their involvement injects into my job search is a positive influence, albeit, from my perspective, a surplus one because I would not purposely wreck any opportunities anyway. The fact that such external influence is present should assure the respondents and the tribunal.

Even when agents want me to pursue opportunities that I think are inappropriate, I go along with their wishes and pursue them anyway. An example of this is the Audit Manager vacancy at CNT Baripas, a European financial institution, which an agent approached me about on 15th June 2007. The documentary evidence shows that even though I explained to the agent that I do not possess the relevant knowledge and experience to perform the role, the agent still wanted to put me forward to the employer. I respected his wish and worked with him. On 13th July, an officer of CNT Baripas interviewed me for the vacancy. During the interview, he informed me that he would not be progressing my application any further because I do not possess sufficient knowledge in the field of compliance to be able to perform the role at a managerial level. The venture was not completely futile, though. The officer told me that I had impressed him and said he would recommend me to the risk departments in CNT Baripas, where he thinks my profile will be more appropriate. Another example is the ALM Quantitative Analyst vacancy at Llords Bank, a UK financial institution, which another agent approached me about on 31st

January 2007. The documentary evidence shows that, again, even though I explained to the agent that I do not possess what it takes to perform the role, he still wished to put me forward for it. Again, I respected his wish and worked with him. On 13th February, an officer of Llords interviewed me for the vacancy. At the end of the interview, she informed me that she would not be pursuing my application any further because my area of expertise is different to the one required for the role. Again, the venture was beneficial, though. She too told me that she is impressed by me and would enquire whether there are any other roles at Llords that might be suitable for me.

If an agent manages to obtain an offer of employment on my behalf, then I will simply accept it, even if I think the job is not right for me. I will not reject any offer, because doing so will deny the agent the commission he would earn, and I would risk alienating him and cutting myself off from employment opportunities.

Internet websites dedicated to recruitment in the financial sector add further support to my testimony that recruitment agencies are the gatekeepers to vacancies suitable for me. Virtually all of the job adverts Neil sent me from the eFinanceJobs website are placed by agencies, not by employers. The adverts do not reveal the identities of the underlying employers. Responding to the adverts amounts effectively to nothing more than initiating contact with the agencies that placed them. The website is essentially a place agents use to market themselves in order to build up their databases of registered candidates. For example, page 904 of the evidence bundles shows an advert from the website for a vacancy with the following description: job title, *"Internal Audit, Investment*

Banking"; seniority level, *"Vice President"*; and salary range, *"£50,000 to £70,000 per annum"*. I applied for this vacancy on 22nd May 2007 by responding to the advert. When the recruitment agency that placed the advert contacted me, I soon learned there actually is not any vacancy underlying the advert. The advert was a dummy the agency had placed with the aim of expanding its database of registered candidates. It was placed merely to fish for new candidates by enticing them to make contact. My application merely resulted in the agency registering me as a new candidate and then, getting on with processing me with a view to finding me a job to earn itself a fee. I can achieve this same result without using the website, by contacting agents directly.

I registered myself on the eFinanceJobs website on 8th January 2007. I did so only in order to address the criticism the respondents subjected me to, of not having made use of it, not because I actually believe I need to register on it. I then proceeded to apply for many of the vacancies that were advertised on it. The only result I achieved was to become registered with more and more recruitment agencies. This is how I became registered with an additional twenty-three agents during the adjournment period of the remedy hearing. In some cases, I achieved nothing at all because the identities of the agents responsible for the adverts were not revealed, and I did not know whom to chase up when I did not receive a response from anyone.

During the adjournment period of the remedy hearing, I applied for four jobs at the respondent bank. One is the Market Risk Associate vacancy in the Market Risk Control team. It reports into Katia Mykonola. It is the same role that I had tried to get reinstated into. Months later, I saw on the bank's website that the vacancy is still open. I applied for it. The bank rejected me saying my experience and skills are far in excess of those required for the role. Another is the Equity Dealer vacancy in its Financial Markets business. It did not respond to my application. I chased it for a response. Eventually, three months after I applied, it responded saying the vacancy is filled. Another is the Model Validation Analyst vacancy, which is also in the bank's Market Risk Department. Again, it did not respond to me. Again, I chased it for a response. Eventually, four months after I applied, it responded saying it is unable to proceed with my application because the vacancy has been put on hold due to, *"business reasons"*. The final one is the Auditor role. Even though I chased the bank for a response, it never responded to me. Effectively, the bank refused all four of my job applications.

I also approached a number of the bank's key officers and offered to work in their departments on a voluntary basis, without pay. I took this initiative because I believe prospective employers will view me positively if I am engaged in some kind of relevant work, rather than sitting around doing nothing. I believe it would improve my chances of finding another job and mitigating my loss. One officer I approached is the Chief Risk Officer. He is responsible for the bank's various Risk departments, such as, Market Risk, Credit Risk, and Compliance Risk. Simon Ong reports into him. Another officer is the Director of the Financial Markets Division. He is responsible for the bank's business division in which the Market Risk Control team resides. Another is a senior member of the Product Control department. The bank refused all three of my requests for voluntary work. On 31st May 2007, the bank's Human Resources department wrote to me saying the bank does not operate a scheme for voluntary work and is unable to entertain my requests.

I have given the respondents so many opportunities to collaborate sensibly with me to enable me to mitigate my loss, and even to pre-empt financial compensation altogether. Right at the beginning of the remedy hearing, I opted for reinstatement, by which I kicked compensation out of play. It is the respondents who brought compensation back into play, by failing to comply with the tribunal's reinstatement orders. Then, I applied for four vacancies advertised on the bank's website. I made three requests to work for the bank on a voluntary basis, to try to improve my employability. Each and every time I approach the respondents, they simply refuse me. I am at a loss as to what else I can do to avoid financial compensation. The respondents scupper my attempt to mitigate my loss fully by wilfully failing to comply with the reinstatement orders without good cause. Then, when I approach them, they do not lift even a finger to allow me to mitigate my loss. But still, they criticise me eagerly for not making enough effort to mitigate it. By their failure to comply with the reinstatement orders, they leave me out on the job market and bring into play four specific factors that seriously damage my chances of finding another job. The factors would never come into play if they reinstate me.

One factor is the issue surrounding my departure from my job. In virtually every recruitment process I go through, at some stage or another, I am asked why I left my job? This is simply just one of the standard questions prospective employers tend to ask. The respondent bank asks this question too. On its online job application form, which I have supplied in the bundles of evidence, it asks applicants for their reasons for leaving each and every employer they ever worked for. In my circumstances, the answer to why I left my job with the respondents is neither trivial, nor is it one which prospective employers wish to hear because it is fraught with negativity.

The long time period of sixteen months for which I am unemployed is another factor affecting adversely my ability to gain employment. In virtually every job interview I attend, I am asked what I have been doing since being dismissed? This also is just a standard question employers tend to ask. When the respondent bank recruited me, its Human Resources department required me to explain each and every gap in my employment history. It reserved the right to investigate further any explanations I gave it, and to dismiss me summarily, if it discovered any issues. Prospective employers want to know what I have been doing since being dismissed. They question why I have been unable to secure another employment in such a long time period. They express concerns rooted in me having been out of work for so long. The truthful answer, that, *I have been trying very hard throughout the whole of the time to find another job, but have been unsuccessful so far*, is not one that inspires them to hire me.

Justifying why I wish to change career from market risk is another factor affecting negatively my ability to gain employment. When I apply for vacancies outside of market risk, employers question my motivation for changing career. This too is a standard question employers tend to ask. I need to justify my motivation for applying for the vacancies because they are different to the ones my career history and profile demonstrate interests in. Despite my best efforts, employers remain unconvinced against the history of a successful, yet prematurely halted, nine-year career in market risk, which I did not leave voluntarily and which I tried to return to via reinstatement. They see I did not leave market risk willingly, out of a genuine desire from within to change career, but was pushed out by external forces beyond my control.

The other factor affecting adversely my ability to get a job is that I litigated against my former employers. I believe prospective employers are shunning me because of this. This is hardly surprising when the, *"best practice employer"*, respondents themselves refuse to reinstate me for exactly this reason. I believe many employers decide not to pursue my job applications purely because I litigated against my former employers, but they do not disclose this genuine reason of theirs because they know it is unlawful. Instead, they give alternative disingenuous, but lawful, reasons that they know they can get away with safely. This is a very difficult thing for me to be able to evidence to the tribunal because, unlike the respondents who made their reason boldly known before the tribunal, other employers are discreet. I am able to provide documentary evidence, though, of five reactions of agents and employers that I experienced since the liability hearing that support my belief.

First, an officer of Hayez, one of the recruitment agencies in my field, contacts me in response to my application to it for the Finance Risk Analyst vacancy it advertised. Everything goes well and the officer seems keen, until he learns that I litigated against my former employers.

Then, he informs me that he needs to seek approval from his superiors as to whether or not the agency can accept me as a candidate. He does not come back to me with an answer. Whenever I chase him up, he responds ambiguously and inconclusively. Eventually, he ceases to respond altogether. The fact that I litigated against my former employers seems to be a significant issue for the agency, sufficient for it to want to have nothing to do with me whatsoever.

Second, when I applied for the Risk Manager vacancy at Mayfair Asset Managers, a hedge fund institution, it enquires why I left my job with the respondents? I tell it the reasons. I do not hear from it again. After some chasing up on my part for a response, it eventually responds asking me why I have not managed to find another job in the year since my dismissal, and what have I been doing since? I respond to its queries, but I never hear from it again. I believe the institution was initially eager and enthusiastic about me as a suitable candidate, but then went off me when it discovered I litigated against my former employers.

Third, when I applied through a recruitment agency for the Auditor Banking vacancy at Argobank, a European banking institution, the bank interviews me for the role. Several weeks later, the agent informs me the bank reported back to him saying I am a good candidate with an interesting profile, I would add an extra dimension to its team, but it would not be pursuing my application any further because it does not think I possess any knowledge of auditing. The agent tells me he thinks the bank's final remark is odd and inconsistent with its preceding remarks, given that I am a qualified Chartered Accountant and have enough knowledge and experience of Auditing for the role. I believe Argobank is initially keen on me, but then, shuns me on learning that I litigated against my former employers, and proffers disingenuous reasons for rejecting my application.

Fourth, I registered my CV with Leibermann Brothers, an American financial institution, for any suitable job opportunities that might arise within it. Leibermann's Human Resources officer contacts me by phone regarding the CAD2 Market Risk Manager vacancy it is recruiting for. During the phone call, she delves into my salary and bonus history. She enquires about my future pay expectations. She seeks to understand the type of position I am looking for. She asks why I left my job? She asks why my final bonus at the bank is significantly lower than the previous year's award? I answer all of her queries during the phone-interview. Immediately after the phone-interview, she follows up with an email asking me to confirm in writing, by return email, the oral responses I gave her during the call, giving as much information as possible on each query. I comply with her request. Then, I do not hear back from her. I chase her up for a response. Eventually, she responds saying my application is unsuccessful because there are other stronger candidates. I think her response is unreasonable and insincere because I believe she initially pursued me because my CV impressed her. I am one of the best candidates on the job market for the vacancy, deserving of a face-to-face interview at the very least. My thoughts are reinforced when, a few days later, a recruitment agent representing Leibermann Brothers for the very same vacancy approaches me for it. I inform the agent that Leibermann has already considered and rejected me. I mention Leibermann's feedback. The agent is surprised by the feedback.

She says she thinks the feedback is unreasonable because she considers me to be a very strong candidate for the role, worthy of an interview, which is why she approached me. Nine other recruitment agencies also approach me for this very same vacancy. Conceivably, I am a strong candidate for the role and worthy of serious consideration. I believe Leibermann Brothers wants nothing to do with me on learning that I litigated against my former employers, and proffers disingenuous reasons for rejecting me.

Fifth, when I applied for the Risk vacancy at Golden Rock, a hedge fund institution, through a recruitment agent, the agent interviews me initially and then progresses my application to an interview with the company. During the interview, Golden Rock's officer dwells unnecessarily deeply, and for far too long a time, on the circumstances relating to my departure from my job with the respondents. He asks deep questions that are surplus to recruitment needs. After the interview, the agent informs me Golden Rock reported back to him saying I am a strong candidate for its vacancy, its officer enjoyed meeting me, my interview technique is very good, but they would be continuing their search for another candidate. Despite good feedback, the organisation decides, for no apparent reason, to continue its search. I believe Golden Rock is put off me by the fact that I litigated against my former employers.

The respondents' failure to reinstate me exacerbates my predicament. The four factors it brings into play severely damage my chances of securing another job. If the respondents reinstate me, as ordered, and as I am still willing to be, then the whole issue of mitigation and finding another job vanishes. Then, none of the detrimental factors I am experiencing on the job market come into being.

I am able to evidence with documents one hundred and twelve jobs that I applied for during the adjournment period of the remedy hearing. I was considered for more jobs though, but I am unable to evidence them with documents because of the informal and oral nature of the recruitment processes concerning them. I applied for a diverse range of roles. They span across a variety of disciplines and fields, including, market risk, risk control, risk management, risk reporting, risk consultancy, risk sales, financial control, product control, pricing control, valuation control, auditing, and other fields. All of my applications were unsuccessful.

Although I found eleven job opportunities to apply for prior to the discrimination liability hearing, only three of them are commensurate with my profile in terms of seniority. One is an internal opportunity at the respondent bank, namely the Head of Derivative Products Risk role in its Market Risk Department. The other two are from the external job market, namely, the role heading up a risk team in the Market Risk department of CEFP, and the Operations Manager vacancy at Tick-It.

Although I applied for at least one hundred and twelve jobs after the liability hearing, compared to eleven before it, still, only two out of the one hundred and twelve are commensurate with my profile in terms of seniority.

One is the Project Management Officer vacancy at Jeffersons International, an American financial institution. I applied for it on 6th February 2007 via the recruitment agency representing it. Even though project management is a completely different field and discipline from my area of expertise, and one that I have not worked in before, I believe I possess skills that make me suitable for the role. On 21st February, the agent informed me that Jeffersons has put its recruitment process for the vacancy on hold.

The other one is the Senior Business Controller role at Scandia Financial Products, a Scandinavian financial institution. I applied for it on 16th February 2007, via the recruitment agency representing it. The role's primary objective is to monitor Scandia's business performance and to challenge its business plans for robustness and appropriateness. This too is a different field from my area of expertise, and one in which I do not have the level of experience that an employer would expect from a candidate for a senior position. Although I have never worked in this field before, I believe I possess transferable skills that make me suitable for the role. On 22nd February, the agent informed me Scandia has, without giving any feedback, decided not to invite me for an interview.

In the period prior to the liability hearing, using only *three agents*, I found *two jobs* on the external job market that are commensurate with my profile. Then, in the period after the liability hearing, using *twenty-six agents*, I still only found *two jobs* that are commensurate with my profile. In the entire period since being told I am selected for dismissal, I did not manage to find a single vacancy on the job market in market risk that matches my profile in terms of experience and seniority. Senior vacancies of any sort in the financial services sector rarely make their way on to the external job market, let alone senior vacancies specifically in market risk. My strategy after the liability hearing, of applying for as many jobs as I can find, regardless of the fact that they do not match my profile, demonstrates two things. First, the job market is buoyant only with vacancies that are too junior for me. Second, whether or not I apply for such vacancies is irrelevant because my profile does not match the employers' requirements, and employers take great care to ensure a good fit. Applying for lots of junior jobs after the liability hearing does not denote any inadequacy in my prior job search. The strategy of applying for lots of junior jobs is *over and above* my legal duty to take reasonable steps to mitigate my loss. I took this step only to address the criticisms the respondents made of me at the initial compensation hearing, in January. I should not be expected to apply for jobs that do not match my profile. Regardless of how many recruitment agents I register with, regardless of whether I register on the eFinanceJobs website, and regardless of how many junior roles I apply for, the *quality* of my job search after the liability hearing remains the same as it was before it, when I was registered with only three agents and applied for jobs that more closely matched my profile. My job search after the liability hearing with twenty-six agents identified only two credible job opportunities, as did my job search prior to the hearing with only three agents. The best opportunity I have of getting back into employment is through reinstatement, to which I am still open.

If I were not dismissed, then I would consider roles at the same level as Neil's. I would not even need to consider, let alone actually apply for, any of the vacancies I chased after to try to mitigate my loss. I have tried to get back into employment through a variety of roles, but I find it very difficult because the respondents' failure to reinstate me renders me severely disadvantaged on the job market. In light of the continuing lack of success I am having in finding another job in the financial sector, despite the tremendous effort I am making, I am forced to consider other careers.

On 18th May 2007, I applied for a place on a *Post Graduate Certificate in Education*, a PGCE, in Secondary School Mathematics at the University of Education in London, which starts in September. The PGCE is a one-year, full-time teacher-training course. Successful completion will enable me to gain employment as a secondary school mathematics teacher from September 2008. The university interviewed me on 28th June. On 4th July, it made me an offer of a place for this year. The course begins in just a few days time. The offer was valid for fourteen days only. I accepted it on 16th July, in order not to lose it due to it expiring. Even having accepted it, I continued as normal with my job search in order to try to mitigate my loss further.

Before my dismissal, I was enjoying a career in banking that was still progressing and had plenty of capacity for progression. It had not peaked. There was substantial room for further progression. I expected my career to continue to climb for quite some time into the future. There was potential to progress to positions equivalent in seniority to Neil's, the various Head of Risk roles. Then, it could progress to positions equivalent to Simon Ong's, the head of department roles. Then, it could progress higher still, to roles equivalent to a Chief Risk Officer's. I was only thirty-nine years old at the time of my dismissal. I had plenty of years of working-life before me. I expected my salary and bonuses to increase accordingly as my career progressed. Simon Ong received a bonus of

£600,000 for 2005, on top of his base salary. The respondents' failure to comply with the reinstatement orders robs me of my ability to earn salaries and bonuses associated with the banking sector. It also robs me of my highly beneficial *final-salary* pension scheme, which is irreplaceable in the financial services sector because employers have ceased to make them available to new employees.

I believe I am entitled to be compensated in full for the damages I suffer because I have discharged my legal duty to mitigate my loss.

'Yes,' I reply.

My counsel gives way to the respondents' counsel to cross-examine me.

'You possess a Computer Engineering degree and an MBA from a London university,' she says. 'You are a qualified Chartered Accountant'.

'That's correct,' I confirm.

'Your employment history shows you move jobs every three years, on average,' she says.

'Three years may well be the mathematical average,' I reply, 'but I worked at UBE for six and a half years. I was at the respondent bank for four and a half years, a duration that I didn't bring to an end and which would have continued longer, had the respondents not ended it'.

'To switch employers approximately every three years is quite the norm in your line of work,' she says.

'My specific career history shows I switched jobs and employers more frequently when I was junior,' I reply. 'That's normal then, to qualify and gain experience. For example, to qualify as a Chartered Accountant takes a minimum of three years. At the start of my career, I stayed three and a half years at the accountancy firm I qualified with. As soon as I qualified, I looked to move on to the next stage of my career. As I became established and senior, my time with employers increased accordingly.

That's normal too'.

'You were a band C employee at the bank,' she says.

'That's correct,' I confirm.

'The data for band C and D employees shows an annual turnover rate of forty-six per cent,' she says. 'Does a staff turnover rate of forty-six per cent surprise you?' she asks.

'There are two points the tribunal should note here,' I answer. 'First, the forty-six per cent rate you refer to is calculated based on a population of staff across the whole of the bank. I worked in the bank's *investment banking* business. It employs only two per cent of its total workforce and is very different in nature from its *retail high street* business, which employs the other ninety-eight per cent. My overall point is, if the tribunal focuses on statistics based on populations that don't apply to me specifically, then it can be misled. This leads on to my second point. The statistic is calculated based on a population of staff who all *resigned* from their jobs voluntarily. I didn't resign; I was *dismissed*. This is an example of a statistic that doesn't apply to me at all because I don't belong in the population on which it is based'.

'The *average length of service* for an employee in the bank's investment banking business, being the business specific to you, is five years,' she says.

'Again, five years may well be the mathematical average,' I reply. 'But, the investment banking business consists of all sorts of employees. Some are junior, at the beginning of their careers, and still trying to find their feet. Others are senior, more established in theirs, and settled. The five-year average paints everyone with the same brush. There are individuals who serve for much shorter time periods than the five-year average, and there are others who serve for considerably longer. For example, Neil has been at the bank for over twelve years now'.

'Moving on,' she says. 'Email correspondence between

a recruitment agent and you shows you attend an interview at another financial institution in the early part of 2005, whilst you are still in the respondents' employment'.

'It wasn't an interview,' I clarify, 'it was a meeting. You cross-examined me on it during the liability hearing. It's already been investigated'.

'You are sufficiently interested in leaving the respondents' employment for you to approach the institution,' she says.

'As I said at the liability hearing, I didn't approach them,' I reply. 'Their agent, a headhunter, approached me entirely without any solicitation on my part, and invited me to meet his client'.

'You attend because you wish to leave your employment,' she says.

'No, that's incorrect,' I reply.

'You do indeed wish to leave because otherwise, attending would be an entirely futile exercise,' she says.

'That's incorrect,' I reply. 'The meeting could validate and assure me of the employment I'm in. If I were offered something sufficiently tempting though, say a promotion and a significant pay rise, then I'd give it serious consideration. I saw no reason not to go and take a look. No specific job was ever communicated to me, not before the meeting, not during it, and not after. The meeting focused on getting to know me. It was networking. Networking is quite normal. Nothing more ever come of it'.

Addressing the respondents' counsel, the chairman interjects, 'the tribunal accepts headhunting and networking activity occurs on a tentative basis. If the prospective employer offered, say, to double his salary, then, of course, he might very well be interested in moving'.

'Yes, Sir,' she replies. 'Moving on, then,' she resumes. 'Why do you leave your previous employment, at CEFP, after a period of only six months?'

'The job turned out not to be as I expected,' I answer. 'After persevering with it for six months, being a reasonable amount of time to be able to make a proper assessment, and after banking my annual bonus safely, I decided to move on'.

'Clearly, you do not like the job,' she says. 'Is it because of technical aspects or because you do not get on with the people?'

'It was entirely because of technical aspects,' I answer. 'The automated systems I relied on to perform some of my duties were so poor that I had to compensate for the deficiencies with laborious manual interventions, which meant working ninety hour weeks. I regularly left the office at midnight, and was back at my desk again just six hours later, by six o'clock in the morning. Sometimes, I worked even past midnight. I even had to come in some weekends too, to compensate for the systems. My kind of job doesn't pay any overtime hours. My job is my responsibility, no matter how long it takes me to do it. From a physical and practical perspective, these sorts of working hours are unsustainable for long periods. There were no plans to improve the systems for at least another two years. My departure had nothing to do with poor relationships. I left on very good terms. My employer tried very hard to persuade me to stay'.

'Under what circumstances do you leave your employment prior that one, at UBE?' she asks.

'I wasn't looking to move,' I answer. 'A headhunter representing CEFP approached me. CEFP offered to double my remuneration package and promote me to the higher corporate title of Vice President. It was good for me. I accepted'.

'Had you flagged up any interest in moving,' she asks.

'No,' I answer. 'The headhunter approached me entirely without any solicitation on my part. I was headhunted'.

'How were you recruited into the Market Risk

Controller role in the respondents' Market Risk Department?' she asks.

'I was voluntarily unemployed at the time, having decided to leave CEFP and take a career-break to relax and travel a bit,' I reply. 'A recruitment agent representing the respondent bank approached me with the Market Risk Controller role. I decided to pursue the opportunity and got the job'.

'Moving on to you surviving waves of redundancies at your employers,' she says. 'Do you feel you avoided redundancy fortuitously or on merit?'

'I was exposed to the risk of redundancy in most years of my employment in investment banking,' I answer. 'Surviving just one or two times might be lucky. Surviving every time must be more than simply luck, it's on merit'.

'Do you accept restructuring and redundancy are facts of life?' she asks.

'Yes, I do,' I answer. 'As I just said, there were redundancies at my employers in most years of my career in banking'.

'Then, it will not surprise you if I tell you the bank has disbanded its Market Risk Control department since your dismissal,' she says. 'So, you see, Mr Singh, you would be made redundant by now, anyway'.

'Oh, really?' I reply in sarcastic tone. 'I'm amazed. I find your claim *impossible* to believe, not least because the FSA, the UK financial regulator, would never permit the bank to conduct its business without practising market risk control'.

'Er, moving on,' she says with such haste that it not only makes obvious her attempt to deceive, but also confirms its failure.

Addressing her, the chairman enquires, 'has the bank actually disbanded its Market Risk Control department?'

'Er,' she stalls. She turns around, confers with Neil in private whispers, and then answers, 'no, Sir. I apologise. My error, I misunderstood'.

But, her charade of a conference with Neil is unconvincing.

'Yes, of course, you misunderstood,' the chairman says in sarcastic tone, rolling his eyes.

Her face reddens.

'Continue,' the chairman instructs her.

'Do you agree,' she resumes, 'that the quality of dealings you have with Neil and other staff cannot be described as harmonious?'

'No, I don't agree,' I answer. 'I certainly did have professional disagreements with Neil and others. But, having professional disagreements isn't disharmonious. Part of my job was to challenge and confront the causes of risk issues, regardless of what or who the causes are, even if they are my line manager or other members of staff. It was also my job to speak up and, if necessary, to disagree. My dealings with everyone were professional. Challenging people in a professional manner, in the performance of my job, isn't disharmonious, it's harmonious'.

'Your manner of interaction with Neil during the course of your employment shows you have a low level of respect for him,' she says.

'That's incorrect,' I reply.

'Page 317 of the evidence bundles shows you send him an email challenging him on a risk control matter,' she says.

'Yes,' I reply. 'I challenged him because my job required me to challenge him, not because I have a low level of respect for him'.

'Your direct and blunt tone in the email is not one a subordinate should use to address a more senior officer,' she says. 'Your interactions show you have a personal relationship issue with him'.

'My tone *is* direct and blunt,' I confirm. 'It's also entirely professional. That's how we communicate in my profession. There's nothing unacceptable about it. Katia communicates with him in the same tone. Controlling market risks and challenging others, even if they are my superiors, was part of my job description. I challenged Neil entirely out of a professional requirement and I did so in professional tone. I didn't have any personal relationship issue with him. I challenged other too in the same way. I didn't have any personal relationship issues with them either'.

'Page 479 of the evidence bundles shows he sends you an email instructing you to keep him informed on a particular matter,' she says. 'You respond saying you will keep him informed in accordance with the established risk procedures. Not only is your response to his instruction terse, but also you fail to act on his instruction'.

'The bank's *Market Risk Control Framework Manual* documents in precise detail the procedures concerning who is to be notified, of what, when, and how,' I reply. 'The procedures stipulate how Neil is to be kept informed, if at all. They're established formally by the bank. They're approved officially by: Simon Ong, Neil's manager; and the FSA, the UK regulator. I always kept Neil informed in accordance with the official procedures. I don't believe I should circumvent them on his instruction just because he's my manager. If he wishes things to be done differently, then he needs to get the procedures changed accordingly, through the formal channels that are available for the purpose, rather than try to achieve his aims through informal backdoors, which might circumvent or undermine some stakeholders' interests'.

'Your tone is very curious for someone who respects his manager,' she says.

'That's incorrect,' I reply. 'I respected him. I also respected the official operating procedures'.

'There are many emails before the tribunal in which you challenge him,' she says. 'Your direct tone of address in all of them shows you have no respect for him as your superior officer. If you did have any, then you would not challenge him as you do'.

'I did respect him,' I reply. 'I also respected the operating control framework, the purpose of which is to safeguard the interests of the stakeholders. My acts of challenging him on risk related issues don't signify I disrespect him. My job was to address risk control issues and to challenge wherever necessary. My motive behind my challenges was never personal, it was always a business motive, being the need to ensure risk control is practised the way the bank and the FSA intend it to be practised'.

The chairman interjects, 'Mr Singh, by *motive*, do you mean you had no intention to be disrespectful towards Mr Hobson?'

'That's correct,' I answer.

'Nevertheless,' the chairman says, 'even in professional conduct, it is still possible to be perceived as being disrespectful. Just because you did not intend to be disrespectful does not mean you are not perceived as being disrespectful'.

'I agree,' I reply. 'I can't control how someone chooses to perceive me. But, Neil never perceived me as being disrespectful. If he did, then he would have had words with me and noted it down on my record. He didn't even record anything to that effect in my very final appraisal, where he criticises me wrongfully. The respondent's have only started saying I disrespect him since the matter of remedy came into play'.

The chairman signals the respondents' counsel to continue.

'You subvert the normal manager and subordinate relationship deliberately,' she resumes.

'That's incorrect,' I reply.

'Your responses to him are hostile and ill-judged reactions to his instructions and comments,' she says.

'I was doing the job the bank gave me to do,' I reply.

'The real point is you have a contemptuous attitude towards him and do not feel he has the right to manage you,' she says.

'That's incorrect,' I assert.
'You have difficulty working under him,' she says.
'That's incorrect,' I answer.
'Continuing to work under him becomes untenable for you,' she says.
'That's incorrect,' I reply.
'You become so disenchanted you wish to leave your employment,' she says. 'This is the true reason why you requested voluntary redundancy in 2004'.
'I never requested voluntary redundancy,' I assert.
'You did request it!' she rebuts aggressively.
'I didn't,' I reply. 'The subject of voluntary redundancy was explored in great depth during the liability hearing. Going through it again now is completely unnecessary and wholly unjustifiable. It wastes valuable tribunal time and increases my legal costs, which I can ill afford. We ran out of time at the January hearing to conclude matters. We had an eight-month delay to reconvene here to continue. I don't want to run out of time again and suffer more delays and costs'.
'Mr Singh!' the chairman interjects sternly. 'You are here to answer questions, not to voice protests! Stick to answering questions!'
'Yes, Sir,' I reply.
Addressing the respondents' counsel, the chairman says, 'the tribunal has accepted Mr Singh's account on the matter. Move on'.
'Moving on, then,' she says. 'You set Neil right in blunt terms on so many occasions. Exactly who is managing whom?'
'That's also been explored in great detail during the liability hearing,' I reply. 'The answer is still the same. He had *management* authority over me, but not *operational* authority. He had the management authority to allocate resources to me, monitor and assess my performance, and to hire and fire me. He didn't have the operational authority to instruct me on how to control risks. I set him

right on operational matters only, being the area on which I had the authority. I did that because to do so was part of my job description. Simon Ong delegated his own operational authority directly to Katia and me, bypassing Neil altogether. The FSA approved the manner of delegation'.

'Your answer is convoluted and disingenuous,' she says.

'It might seem convoluted to the naïve onlooker who isn't familiar with the setup,' I reply, 'but, it certainly isn't disingenuous. The setup is documented clearly in the bank's procedures manuals, which are supplied to the tribunal, and which were investigated in detail during the liability hearing'.

'Page 418 of the evidence bundles shows Neil sends you an email regarding a risk control matter, in which he instructs you to make a specific type of formal notification to the FSA,' she says. 'You make a different notification altogether. Your defiance of his instruction is a *coded* criticism of him'.

'It's correct I made a different notification,' I reply, 'but, it's incorrect I made it to criticise him. I made it because it was the correct one to make. There's no coded message. The situation exemplifies the fact that I had operational authority, like to determine the types of formal notifications to make to the FSA, and he didn't. The type of notification to be made was my responsibility, not his. Simon Ong delegated his operational authority concerning formal notifications to the FSA directly to Katia and me. It was my responsibility to make the correct notification, regardless of what Neil says. If a notification error occurred, then Simon would hold me accountable for it, not Neil. The accountability is clearly documented as being mine alone, not Neil's also'.

'Your regard for him as someone who is failing wholly in his management responsibilities, and your role as being one to set him right in blunt terms, cannot be more manifest,' she says.

'He had management authority over me,' I reply. 'I never challenged or set him right on his management authority. The direct and blunt terms are merely symptomatic of the very dynamic, real-time environment we operate in. Financial markets are highly volatile. Sometimes, situations or opportunities may exist only for a brief window of time. I need to act fast, which means I need to communicate quickly, concisely, and effectively. That means using direct, imperative language. The environment simply doesn't allow for the time needed to compile overly polite communications loaded with superfluous, indirect, deferent, subservient, submissive language. We just don't behave like that in my profession. The trading floor is not a place where one would say things like, *dear Mr Hobson, thank you for your email, with the greatest of respect, after much consideration, in my humble opinion, I should be grateful if.* We get directly to the point'.

'You propose your team ought to report directly into Simon Ong,' she says. 'You do this in order to circumvent Neil'.

'It's correct I proposed it,' I reply, 'but, it's incorrect I did it to circumvent Neil. Simon had established and approved risk control procedures in which Neil didn't feature between himself and us. Simon had excluded him. It's impossible for me to circumvent him when Simon's already excluded him. Yes, I made the proposal about the reporting line. I did it to address the regular occurrences of operational issues. I was not alone in making the proposal. The previous Head of Market Risk Control and Katia also proposed exactly the same'.

'Your answer is a flimsy justification for a way to bypass Neil,' she says in aggressive tone. 'An attempt on your part to circumvent him is exactly how he perceives your proposal to be'.

'My explanation is frank and sincere,' I reply. 'The matter of the reporting line proposal also was explored in great depth during the liability hearing'.

'You being troubled by having to report into him cannot be more manifest,' she says. 'It surely paints the picture of unhappiness on your part to the extent that you wish to leave your employment'.

'That's incorrect,' I reply. 'I was very happy in my job. If operational issues arose, then my job was to deal with them, which included confronting the causes and proposing solutions. Confronting issues and their causes, that is, doing my job, doesn't mean I'm unhappy and want to leave; it means I'm getting on with my job'.

'The stream of email correspondence indicates you are uncomfortable in your employment with the respondents,' she says.

'That's incorrect,' I reply. 'It actually indicates I carried out the job the bank gave me to do'.

'You were managed directly by Simon Ong before being managed by Neil,' she says.

'Immediately before Neil, I was managed by the then Head of Market Risk Control,' I clarify. 'Before that, Simon Ong managed me directly, and the other two members of my team'.

'Who conducts your 2003 mid-year performance appraisal?' she asks.

'Simon,' I reply.

'He awards you a performance rating of 5/8,' she says.

'That's correct,' I reply.

'Do you feel a rating of 5/8 is justified?' she asks.

'I felt it didn't reflect my level of performance accurately,' I answer. 'I believed I deserved a rating of 6/8, like I had achieved in every one of my previous appraisals'.

'Do you feel you are assessed fairly, even though you feel you deserve a higher rating?' she asks.

'I thought I deserved a higher rating,' I answer.

The chairman interjects, 'Mr Singh, did you accept Mr Ong could have a different perception to yours, even if you disagree with his?'

'Yes,' I answer. ' I accepted there's some subjectivity involved in assessing performance and that there's room for a difference of opinion'.

'Could you see why Mr Ong might have his particular view?' the chairman asks.

'Yes, I could,' I answer, 'because I took the matter up with him and he explained his reasons to me'.

The chairman signals the respondents' counsel to continue.

'Do you find the way he assesses you to be troublesome?' she resumes.

'I thought his assessment underrated my performance,' I answer. 'So, I discussed the matter with him. Having taken the step of discussing it with him and heard his reasoning, which I accepted, I felt I achieved satisfactory closure on the matter. I moved on untroubled'.

'Up to December 2003, the Market Risk Control team consisted of three Controllers,' she says. 'You and two others, all reporting into Simon directly'.

'That's correct,' I confirm.

'Then, in December 2003, Simon reorganises your team,' she says. 'He transfers one member out, moving her to another team in the department. Thus, your team shrinks in size to two people, you and the other member'.

'That's correct,' I reply.

'He also creates a new role at the time,' she says, 'the Head of Market Risk Control role, to head up your team, into whom the Controllers in the team will report'.

'That's correct,' I agree.

'He promotes the other team member, your colleague, to the freshly created head vacancy and resets your reporting line into him'.

That's correct,' I confirm.

'Your peer becomes your superior officer,' she says.

'Yes, that's correct,' I reply.

'Do you feel his promotion is appropriate, or is it a cause for some unhappiness on your part?' she asks. 'Do you feel you should be the one who should have been promoted instead?'

'I thought his promotion is entirely appropriate,' I answer. 'I didn't feel any unhappiness about it. Candidates were invited to apply for the Head vacancy. My colleague applied; I didn't. I don't expect to be promoted into a vacancy I didn't apply for, and I don't begrudge someone who applied for it being given it. There was no cause for any unhappiness on my part. I was happy about it'.

'You challenge your final performance appraisal at the bank, in which the tribunal says Neil marked you down unfairly,' she says. 'Not being credited correctly for performances and achievements at the bank affects adversely your level of contentment in your employment'.

'I loved my job,' I reply. 'I didn't want to leave it. I exercised my right to challenge Neil's grossly unfair assessment of my performance to try to flag up and address the issues. That doesn't mean I wanted to leave my job. It shows I cared enough about my employment and my career prospects that I went to the trouble of trying to fix what's wrong. It shows I wanted to stay and make it work'.

'Do you accept Katia's views as being accurate?' she asks. 'She says you are not an easy person to work with. She says you are excessive in the level of your challenge. She says she has to spend considerable time and energy in meetings with you to explain why decisions are being made as they are, in order to try to convince you to agree with the rationales behind them. She says she does not feel the working relationship is as efficient as it could be'.

'We don't know whether or not those are actually her views,' I reply. 'She didn't express them herself. Neil expressed them on her behalf and doesn't provide any independent confirmation from her'.

The chairman interjects, 'Mr Singh, you have not addressed the question fully. Do you doubt Miss

Mykonola expressed such views?'

'I *absolutely* doubt it,' I answer. 'She has no cause, whatsoever, to say what Neil says on her behalf. That's why there isn't any independent confirmation from her'.

The chairman signals the respondents' counsel to continue.

'Moving on,' she resumes. 'During the two-week consultation period relating to your dismissal, you say to Neil and Veronica, *"Whatever happens now, I'm out"*. I put it to you, Mr Singh, by your statement, you *resign* your employment voluntarily and are reconciled with moving on elsewhere'.

'The suggestion that I resigned voluntarily is ridiculous,' I reply. 'I didn't resign. I was dismissed. My statement isn't a reflection of my mind-set of being reconciled to moving on elsewhere. It's a reference to the respondents' decision to dismiss me being final. It's a reference to my fate being sealed when they told me I'm at risk and told the rest of my team their jobs are safe. It's a reference to the meaninglessness of the so-called consultation process being conducted after my fate's already sealed'.

'You also express that to recover from the dismissal will take you between one and two years,' she says. 'Did you take any advice at that stage as to the condition of the job market and how long to recover from the dismissal might take you?' she asks.

'No,' I answer. 'I didn't have the time to take any advice at that stage. It was very early on in the process, and I was bogged down with the issues of unfairness and the so-called consultation process. I have knowledge and experience of the job market myself. I drew on my own understanding. I knew Katia, having been made redundant from her previous job, spent the next eighteen months unemployed, looking for a job, before eventually securing a job with us'.

'At your dismissal, you form the view that the job market is poor,' she says. 'Whom did you consult to form this view?'

'The recruitment agents I'm registered with,' I answer, 'and my personal contacts in the industry, and my own understanding of the industry'.

'A press release at the time from one of the agents you are registered with suggests the job market is very buoyant,' she says.

'The press release you're referring to is very general,' I reply. 'It concerns the job market as a whole being buoyant. I meant the job market specific to my profile is poor'.

'Should the tribunal find puzzling your claim that the job market is poor when your own agent's press release claims it is very buoyant?' she asks.

'Not at all,' I answer. 'There's nothing to be puzzled about. The press release talks generally about the wider job market. I talk about the job market specific to my profile, to market risk roles and market risk professionals'.

'The job market is, in fact, very buoyant,' she asserts. 'The only reason you say it is poor is for posturing, to gain an advantage in negotiating a financial settlement package from the respondents'.

'That's incorrect,' I reply.

'Moving on,' she says. 'The bank arranges its out-placement consultancy to support you in finding another job'.

'That's correct,' I reply.

'You do not avail yourself of the support,' she says.

'That's incorrect,' I reply. 'I availed myself of it. I had two face-to-face consultation meetings with the out-placement consultants. Each one lasted an hour. Each meeting was with the professional consultants assigned to me. The first meeting was at the consultancy's premises in Mayfair. The second was at its offices in the City. In the first month of the support service, I engaged with the consultancy over the phone for a total of about four hours. I attended a networking seminar it organised, and had my

CV reviewed by it'.

'You are entitled to ten hours of support,' she says. 'The amount you take up does not seem to be much'.

'I took up about six hours,' I reply. 'Different people need different amounts of support. The amount of the entitlement I took up was the amount the professional consultants, who are the experts on the matter, agreed is appropriate for me, specifically'.

'Besides the two consultation meetings you refer to,' she says, 'you do not attend any of the other programmes of support the consultancy offers'.

'That's incorrect,' I reply.

'Moving on,' she says. 'Prior to the liability hearing, you use the services of only three recruitment agencies. Thereafter, you use the services of over twenty. Clearly, you are not at all enthusiastic about finding another job before the liability hearing'.

'That's incorrect,' I respond.

'Could you explain to us all what you think your duty to mitigate your loss means?' she asks.

'To take reasonable steps to get the highest paying job I can, as quickly as possible,' I answer.

'Do you agree it means making all reasonable efforts and committing yourself to the task wholeheartedly?' she asks.

'Yes,' I reply.

'Do you agree it means showing yourself to as many employers as possible?' she asks.

'To as many employers as is *reasonably* practical,' I clarify.

'Do you agree it means not to scupper your employment prospects?' she asks.

'Yes,' I answer.

'Prior to the liability hearing, the reason you give to recruitment agents and prospective employers for your dismissal is *redundancy*,' she says.

'That's correct,' I confirm.

'Do you agree employers understand fully that redundancy is a part of normal working life in the City?' she asks.

'Yes,' I answer.

'Do you agree they are not troubled by redundancy being the reason for a dismissal?'

'Yes,' I reply.

'Do you agree the reason of redundancy is not an impediment to finding another employment?' she asks.

'Generally speaking, yes,' I agree.

'No prospective employer will be unsettled by the reason of redundancy,' she says.

'I agree redundancy is *generally* a neutral reason,' I reply.

'After the liability hearing, you give a different reason for your dismissal,' she says.

'That's correct,' I reply. 'The reasons I give now are *unfairness, race discrimination*, and *a failure to comply with reinstatement orders*'.

'Why do you not continue to explain your dismissal simply by redundancy, as you do before the liability hearing?' she asks.

'Before the liability hearing, I gave redundancy as the reason because the official and public reason, then, was redundancy,' I answer. 'The tribunal's rulings changed the official reason. The official reasons became unfairness, race discrimination and a failure to comply with reinstatement orders. I am duty bound to tell agents and employers the official reasons for my dismissal, if they ask me, which they almost always do'.

'Do you think the reasons you give after the liability hearing are likely to unsettle prospective employers?' she asks.

'I don't know for certain how any individual employer will react,' I reply. 'After all, I've done nothing wrong that should cause any of them any concerns about me'.

'Employers might be wary of you for having litigated against your former employers,' she says.

'That's correct,' I reply. 'The respondents' own initial reaction to my request to be reinstated vouches for that possibility. Right here, before the tribunal, they brazenly declared they will not reinstate me because I litigated against them'.

Addressing the respondents' counsel, the chairman interjects, 'the tribunal needs to make its judgment regarding Mr Singh's duty to mitigate his loss on the basis that he does not act *unlawfully* in discharging his duty. Has he acted unlawfully by disclosing that he litigated?'

'I will answer that question in due course, Sir,' she replies. 'I request the tribunal to bear with my approach'.

'If he has not acted unlawfully,' the chairman persists, 'then should he be criticised, the way you criticise him, for disclosing he is the subject of unfairness, race discrimination, and a failure to comply with reinstatement orders?'

'All will become clear in due course, Sir,' she replies. 'I request the tribunal to bear with me'.

'Continue cautiously,' the chairman warns her.

'Do you agree that if you explain your dismissal with unfairness and race discrimination,' she resumes, 'the explanation is likely to kill off all your job prospects?'

'That's just a general assumption,' I answer. 'Employers should not hold the explanation against me. I'm not a wrongdoer'.

'Let me put it to you this way, then,' she says. 'Do you agree that if you explain your dismissal with redundancy instead, then your job prospects will be better?'

'Yes,' I answer.

'Your duty to mitigate your loss includes the duty to give yourself the best prospects of employment,' she says in harsh tone. 'You kill off your prospects purposely because you are looking to the respondents to provide you with an indemnity for an on-going remuneration package'.

'Stop right there!' the chairman interjects sternly addressing her. 'He is only obliged to act reasonably!

Whilst the respondents bear the burden to prove he acts unreasonably, discharging the burden does not entitle them to criticise him excessively! If he explains his dismissal by unfairness and discrimination, then he faces reduced employment prospects. If he explains it by redundancy, then he faces better prospects. The way he explains it has to be looked at in terms of reasonableness on his part'.

'Sir,' she replies in humble tone, 'I am not suggesting he should explain his dismissal with untruths. I am suggesting he can explain it with redundancy and, thereby, enhance his prospects. He gives the explanation that he knows will scupper his prospects. This, by itself, amounts to unreasonableness on his part. Furthermore, if he does not have the prospect of financial compensation before him, then he would act differently. Then, he would advance reasons that improve his employment prospects'.

'Hmm,' the chairman muses leaning back into his chair. Then, sitting up again, he signals her to continue.

'If your circumstances are divorced from the possibility of collecting financial compensation,' she resumes, 'then you would act completely differently towards prospective employers'.

'That's incorrect,' I reply. 'I will act exactly the same way as I do, even if there is no prospect of financial compensation before me'.

The chairman interjects, 'Mr Singh, your duty is to act reasonably. The law suggests that if you act as though you have no possibility of receiving compensation, then you act reasonably. I put it to you, Mr Singh, if you do not have any possibility of receiving compensation from the respondents, then you would explain your dismissal with redundancy, not unfairness and discrimination'.

'Regardless of the prospect of compensation,' I answer, 'I'll explain my dismissal with unfairness, discrimination, and the failure to comply with orders, because these are the official and public reasons for my dismissal now, and

I'm obliged to give the official reasons, if asked'.

The chairman signals the respondents' counsel to continue.

'You,' she resumes, 'volunteer the reasons for your dismissal to agents and employers without the reasons being elicited from you. You want the reasons to be known, to be out there, in order to unsettle employers'.

'I disclosed the reasons on a need-to-know basis only,' I reply. 'Recruitment agents need to know, so they can consider the matter of my dismissal and decide how to address it before they progress me to their clients, the employers. By knowing the reasons, they can pave the way for me, if they wish to, by using their relationships with their clients to prime them to be receptive to me. I didn't volunteer the reasons to employers. I disclosed them to employers only upon being asked for them'.

'The email correspondence with a recruitment agent, on page 445 of the evidence bundles,' she says, 'shows you disclose the reasons for your dismissal to the agent without the agent eliciting them from you'.

'That email relates to my registration with a new agent,' I reply. 'The terms and conditions of the agency's agreement required me to make the disclosure'.

'The email correspondence with another agent, on page 173 of the evidence bundles,' she says, 'one that you are already registered with, shows you disclose the reasons to the agent without the agent eliciting the reasons from you'.

'The agency's formal agreement with me requires me to update them of any changes in my circumstances,' I reply. 'For example, if I change my address, then I need to take it upon myself to update the agent, not wait for the agent to elicit from me whether I've changed my address. Similarly, when the official reasons for my dismissal changed by the tribunal's rulings, I needed to update the agents I'm already registered with. Updating the agent is what I was doing by the email you refer to'.

'Once disclosed to agents,' she says, 'the reasons for

your dismissal become a significant matter at interviews with employers. You go to great pains to make them a large topic of conversation'.

'I go to no pains at all to make my dismissal a topic of conversation,' I reply. 'Why I took up previous employments, and why I left them, are simply standard questions most employers tend to ask me at some stage during the recruitment process'.

Addressing the respondents' counsel, the chairman interjects, 'there is a world of difference between recruitment agents and employers. Agents will not disclose unnecessarily the reasons for his dismissal to prospective employers. Explain to the tribunal why his act of disclosing the reasons to agents makes his dismissal more likely to be discussed at interviews with employers'.

'The answer to that question will become apparent in due course, Sir,' she says. 'I request the tribunal to continue to bear with my approach'.

The chairman permits her to continue.

'Did you instruct the agents to inform employers of the reasons for your departure?' she resumes.

'No,' I reply. 'My responsibility to recruitment agents is to tell them of my circumstances. It's their responsibility to decide how to deal with the information I give them. I didn't instruct them to inform employers'.

'Your email correspondences to recruitment agents, giving them feedback on how interviews you attended with employers went, show the topic of your dismissal is discussed at interviews time after time,' she says.

'Yes, that's correct,' I reply.

'Do you not think,' she asks, 'you ought to stop explaining your dismissal with unfairness, discrimination, and a failure to comply with reinstatement orders, and explain it with redundancy, instead?'

'No,' I answer. 'I'm obliged to answer the questions put to me by the employers honestly, not least because of the terms and conditions of the registration agreements I signed up to with recruitment agents. The agents' registration forms show the specific terms and conditions that bind me. They show I'm obliged to disclose all material matters to them, such as the reasons for my departure from my job. They also show I'm obliged to answer all questions put to me by them and by their clients, the employers, truthfully, accurately and completely. I consulted the agents on how I should address the matter of my dismissal in interviews with employers. They didn't recommend any change in my approach'.

The chairman interjects, 'Mr Singh, are the terms and conditions you signed up to with recruitment agents in the bundles of evidence? Can you direct the tribunal to one such agreement document?'

'Yes,' I answer. 'I've provided the tribunal with every single one of them. Page 291 shows the agreement with one agent, Hutson. Clause 7 of the agreement clearly shows I'm obliged to answer all questions put to me by Hutson, and by its clients, the employers, *"truthfully, accurately, and completely"*.

Reviewing the document, the chairman addresses the respondents' counsel and asks, 'what do you make of the agreement?'

'Hmm,' she contemplates. 'Er, yes, it confirms what he says,' she concedes in frustrated tone.

The chairman signals her to continue.

'The respondents' failure to comply with the reinstatement orders does not form part of the reasons of your dismissal,' she resumes. 'By advancing it as a reason, you volunteer more information than is necessary, by which you achieve nothing other than to give the issue greater prominence. Why do you advance the respondents' failure to comply as a reason?'

'Because,' I answer, 'it's one of the reasons for my departure from the bank. But for the failure to reinstate me, I'd be back in my job. There'd effectively be no dismissal, if the respondents reinstate me'.

'Informing prospective employers that the respondents failed to reinstate you suggests to them that you wish to return to your job,' she says. 'Do you think that induces them to recruit you?'

'I believe the fact that the tribunal ordered reinstatement induces them to recruit me,' I answer, 'because it tells them I'm not at any fault, and I'm capable of closing off issues amicably and reconciling with those who wronged me'.

'You are very keen to ensure recruitment agents have as much information as possible about your dismissal,' she says.

Addressing her, the chairman interjects, 'he has already demonstrated he feels obliged to make certain disclosures to them by the terms and conditions of the agreements he signed up to. Move on'.

'Yes, Sir,' she replies in frustrated tone. 'Your email correspondence to the HR officer of Leibermann Brothers regarding the CAD2 Market Risk Manager vacancy,' she resumes. 'You disclose the unfairness and discrimination. You also disclose the respondents' failure to comply with reinstatement orders. Furthermore, you disclose the bonus being tainted by race discrimination. The amount of information you disclose all points to you getting out a megaphone and shouting it out from the rooftops. The employer does not elicit the information from you. Why do you disclosed it?'

'Because the employer did elicit it from me,' I answer. 'It first elicited it orally during the interview it conducted with me over the phone. Then, it elicited it in writing, in the email you reference. The email shows clearly the HR officer contacted me by phone, firstly, regarding the vacancy, and conducted an over-the-phone interview. During the interview, she asked me why I left each of my previous employments? She asked me about my remuneration history, and questioned why my final bonus at the bank dropped significantly, when every year previously it had risen? I answered all of her questions orally over the phone. Following the phone-interview, she sent me an email asking me to put in writing the answers I had given her'.

'Why do you disclose the bonus being tainted with race discrimination?' she asks.

'Because,' I answer, 'she asked me to explain why my final bonus dropped so significantly compared to the previous year's, to which the answer is because it is tainted with race discrimination'.

'Why do you think it necessary to mention the respondents' failure to comply with reinstatement orders?' she asks.

'I've already told you,' I reply. 'It's one of the reasons for my departure. But for the failure to comply, I'd be back in my job and, effectively, there'd be no dismissal'.

The chairman interjects, 'Mr Singh, would you always disclose the reasons for your dismissal to recruitment agents?'

'Yes,' I answer. 'They always ask me the reasons. They are very thorough. Even if they don't ask, I would still tell them. They need to know in order to perform their part in the process properly, and I'm obliged to make them aware of the reasons by the terms and conditions they make me sign up to. Plus, they'll find out sooner or later, anyway. People know each other in the industry. They talk. Then, I'll be in their bad books for not having told them myself'.

'Would you always answer in terms of unfairness, discrimination, and the failure to comply with reinstatement orders when employers ask you for the reasons for your departure from the respondents, whether they ask you face-to-face, on application forms, or over the phone?' the chairman asks.

'When it comes to employers,' I answer, 'I only say anything on my dismissal *if and when* they ask me. Otherwise, I don't volunteer any information. When they ask me, then, yes, I answer in these terms'.

'Were there any employers who did not ask?' the chairman asks.

'Virtually every employer I engaged with asked me at some stage in their process,' I answer. 'It's just a standard question. There is one employer though, Satsui International, a Japanese financial institution, that didn't ask. It didn't ask and I didn't volunteer anything. Page 471 of the evidence bundles shows this'.

Reviewing page 471, the chairman addresses the respondents' counsel and asks, 'what do you make of the evidence on page 471?'

'Er, it verifies Mr Singh's account,' she concedes.

The chairman signals her to continue.

'Except for this one employer, Satsui International,' she resumes, 'you volunteer the reasons for your dismissal to all other employers prior to the reasons being elicited from you. You do this in order to give the matter particular emphasis in the knowledge that your job prospects will be jeopardised. You do this with a view to collect financial compensation from the respondents'.

'That's incorrect,' I reply. 'I don't do it to jeopardise my prospects, I do it because I need to be honest'.

'Oh! To be honest,' she says in sarcastic tone. 'Why, then, are you not honest prior to the liability hearing? Why do you not disclose to agents and employers, then, that there is a tribunal hearing pending?' she asks.

'I'm obliged to tell them relevant official facts only,' I answer. 'The public fact at the time is that my dismissal is a redundancy. I'm not obliged to tell them I have a dispute going on with my former employers, and that there's a hearing pending. That's *private* at the time and irrelevant to recruitment needs. I only need to tell them about it from when it becomes public'.

Addressing the respondents' counsel, the chairman interjects, 'there is the possibility at the time that the pending hearing might not occur. The dispute might be settled otherwise, or he might change his mind and decide to withdraw from litigation before the hearing occurs. Disclosing there is a hearing pending would not be in his best interest'.

'Moving on, then,' she says. 'Your application for the Head of Derivative Products Risk vacancy in the respondents' Market Risk Department is very telling'.

'I don't know what it's very telling of,' I reply, 'but, I confirm I applied for it. I applied during my notice of termination period to try to save myself from being dismissed'.

'Moving on,' she says. 'You are a highly qualified individual. Yet, you decide to pursue a career in teaching, by which you do not minimise your future loss of earnings'.

'I've done the best I can, given the predicament the respondents have put me in,' I reply.

'You could put your degree in Computer Engineering to good use,' she says.

'I got the degree in 1987,' I reply. 'I haven't worked in computing for twenty years now. Computing's progressed in leaps and bounds since then. I have no computing experience of any value to an employer'.

'If your computing knowledge has atrophied,' she says, 'then the Chartered Accountancy qualification you possess opens up a whole realm of employment opportunities at very much higher levels of remuneration than of a secondary school mathematics teacher'.

'I tried to use my accountancy qualification too,' I reply, 'not least by applying for the Auditor role at the respondent bank, which it never replied back to me on. I didn't manage to secure any employment off the back of my accountancy qualification because I've been out of the profession for over thirteen years'.

'Moving on,' she says. 'The idea that employees are shackled to their employers by deferred bonuses, which are forfeited if they resign voluntarily, is highly fanciful'.

'The bank operates a deferred bonus scheme,' I reply. 'Its terms and conditions are, if employees resign voluntarily, then they forfeit all of their previous two year's deferred earnings it's holding on to. My bonuses were the subject of the scheme. The scheme documents are in the bundles of evidence provided to the tribunal. One effect of the scheme is to deter employees from leaving voluntarily, by making resignation economically unattractive. It also has the effect of making us less attractive to prospective employers, by raising the possibility of them having to make golden hello payments to compensate us for the bonuses we forfeit'.

'The deferred amounts are released and paid to employees if and when they resign,' she says.

'Then, deferring the amounts is an entirely futile exercise,' I assert. 'The scheme documents clearly state the deferred amounts are forfeited if the employee resigns voluntarily'.

'The standard practice in the investment banking sector is for employers to compensate new employees for any accrued bonuses and benefits they might forgo by jumping ship,' she says.

'I know employers sometimes do that,' I reply, 'but, it's on a specific, case-by-case basis only. It's not a standard, general, or routine practice'.

'I have no more questions,' she says.

The chairman invites my counsel to re-examine me.

'What makes you decide to pursue a career in teaching?' my counsel asks.

'Necessity,' I answer. 'I've exhausted all other avenues. I've not found another job. I can't stay jobless indefinitely. I need to get a job. I need to earn a living, for obvious reasons. I look to teaching out of necessity'.

'I have no more questions,' she says.

The chairman invites the judge on his right to cross-examine me.

'What sort of salary might you expect to earn in

teaching?' the judge asks me.

'The government will give me a nine thousand pound training bursary for the PCGE course,' I answer. 'After completing the course, I expect to take up a teaching post paying around twenty-five thousand pounds per annum. I don't expect my pay as a teacher to rise at anywhere near the high rate at which it rose in investment banking. In banking, it went up by around ten per cent year-on-year. As a teacher, I also don't expect to receive any annual bonuses of the same order of magnitude as I received in banking'.

'What was the process for obtaining a place on the PGCE course?' the judge asks.

'First, I completed the university's on-line application form,' I answer. 'Then, the university mailed me some maths tests and exercises that I had to complete and submit. Then, I was invited to attend an assessment day at the university. There, I went through interviews with lecturers and participated in group exercises with other candidates'.

'Did the university ask you why you left the bank?' the judge asks.

'No,' I answer. 'And, I didn't volunteer anything on the matter'.

'Is there any chance you might return at some point in the future to work again in the banking sector?' the judge asks.

'I say there's no chance,' I answer. 'Prospective employers shun me for litigating against my formers employers. This precludes my return. The only real chance I have of returning is if the respondents should decide to reinstate me. But, it's clear that's never going to happen. This factor aside, the fulltime PGCE course, with its very heavy workload, adds to the difficulty of returning. The course demands total commitment. As well as attending lectures, studying, and completing coursework assignments, it also includes lesson planning, teaching, marking, and complying with a substantial amount of administration. All this will consume all of my time, which will keep me away from banking and make it even harder to return'.

'At what point will you feel sufficiently de-skilled not to be able to return to the sector?' the judge asks.

'I don't know for certain,' I answer. 'It's very difficult to say. My skills are already atrophying by being out of the sector for a year and a half now. Employers already question why I haven't managed to find another job in one and a half years. It doesn't look good. The PGCE course will preclude me from working in banking and maintaining my financial experience up to date, which is a significant factor that'll make returning harder, in addition to the other factor I mentioned'.

'I have no more questions,' the judge says.

The chairman invites the judge on his left to cross-examine me.

'Of all the accountancy related jobs you applied for, only one is outside of the banking sector, being to a large professional accountancy practice,' the judge says.

'That's correct,' I reply. 'It's one I applied for directly myself, without any intermediary recruitment agents'.

'Is the Chartered Accountancy qualification you possess current, or out of date?' the judge asks.

'It's current in the sense that I still possess it and pay my annual subscription to the Institute,' I answer. 'I gained it in 1993, though. As soon as I qualified, I moved out of accountancy and into banking, where I've spent my career since. I haven't kept abreast of the developments in accounting. There are new rules and regulations coming out all the time. I'm way behind the curve'.

'What did you do to try to place yourself with recruitment agents who represent accountancy practices?' the judge asks.

'The agents I'm registered with represent accountancy practices also,' I answer. 'But, because of my experience, they pigeonhole me towards accountancy related roles in financial institutions, rather than in accountancy practices'.

'You could ask them to put you forward to accountancy practices,' the judge says.

'I did ask,' I reply. 'But, they don't think I am suitable. They're reluctant to put me forward to their accountancy clients, and I can't force them. They're correct in their assessment because when I applied to the accountancy practice directly myself, it rejected my application virtually immediately. I'm out dated. Accountancy practices would rather recruit a fresh, up-to-date accountant, instead of a stale, out-of-dated one'.

'Did you do anything else to try to pursue a career in accountancy?' the judge asks.

'I applied for numerous vacancies calling for the Chartered Accountancy qualification and related skills,' I answer, 'including an auditing role at the respondent bank. I applied for vacancies in audit, financial control, product control, and valuation control, to mention a few off the top of my head. I tried to use my skills and experiences as far and as best as I could'.

'I have no more questions,' the judge says.

'You inform recruitment agents and employers the reasons for your departure are unfairness, discrimination, and a failure to comply with reinstatement orders,' the chairman resumes. 'Were you advised by anyone to give these reasons?'

'No,' I answer. 'I decided to give these reasons based on some considerations. I believe I need to maintain the agents' and employers' trust and confidence. There's also my own understanding of my obligations arising out of the terms and conditions of the relationships I signed up to. There are my ethics and values too'.

'Did the recruitment agents give you any advice on what to say to employers about your departure from your job?' the chairman asks.

'No,' I answer. 'They went through the matter with me

and were confident I'd approach it sensibly. They're careful. They won't risk putting me before their clients if they think I'm going to reflect badly on them'.

'What do you think might happen if you take up employment with an employer who asks you why you left the bank, but to whom you do not disclose the reasons are unfairness, discrimination and the failure to comply with reinstatement orders?' the chairman asks.

'I can end up in *extremely* difficult and stressful situations,' I answer. Employers ask questions to gain information with which to make their decisions. If I disclose the reasons, then the employer can make a decision based on the information. Then, the employer has no cause to be surprised in the future, like, by leaning the reasons from elsewhere. The employer can have no recourse to me. But, if I don't disclose the reasons, then the employer doesn't have the opportunity to make a decision based on the information. Then, I run the risk of the employer discovering the reasons at some stage in the future from elsewhere. The consequences of that are likely to be very grave on my character, my situation, and my prospects. If you turn to page 291 in the bundles of evidence again, to the terms and conditions I signed up to with Hutson, the recruitment agency, you see clause 8 says, *"if I am employed by a client of Hutson and the information I provided is found to be inaccurate, incomplete, or misleading, my employment may be summarily terminated"*. This means, I can be fired on the spot. Furthermore, finance is a highly regulated sector. The FSA regulates not only financial institutions, but also us individuals, personally. I must maintain complete integrity, otherwise the FSA may preclude employers from employing me and my position will become untenable. The employer would be within its rights to discipline me, and even to dismiss me for misrepresentation or, perhaps, even for fraud'.

6

SARAH RIGSBY'S TESTIMONY

~ Wednesday 22nd August 2007, 2:00 p.m. ~

'Mrs Rigsby, is that your signature on the witness statement and is that the evidence you wish to give?' the respondents' counsel asks her, she having just sworn in at the witness desk.

She has presented the tribunal her statement regarding compensation. It says the following:

> I have worked for the bank for five years. I am a Director of HR. I have overall responsibility for the bank's Financial Markets Risk Division, being the division in which Ranjit Singh worked. I acquired responsibility for the division just a few months ago, in April 2007, a year after Ranjit's dismissal. I had no previous knowledge of his dismissal or of the litigation because the Market Risk Department was not under my remit then.
>
> I recall having a conversation with the Director of the Financial Markets Division, in May 2007, about a request he had received from an individual for an opportunity to undertake voluntary work within the division. I advised him the bank does not have any policy or precedent for taking on voluntary workers. I explained the bank does not take on voluntary workers due to concerns about security of information and the trading floor environment.
>
> Regarding the bank's bonus awards, its bonus scheme is entirely discretionary. It operates in such

a way that an overall amount of money for each division of the bank is accrued into a bonus pot. The amount of accrual depends on the division's performance. Then, the divisional bonus pot is allocated to the various business areas within the division. After that, each business area pot is divided into bonuses for the individuals who work within the area.

In order to determine the accrual in the overall bonus pot for the support areas of the bank, of which the Market Risk Department in which Ranjit worked is one, market data on remuneration from an external source is used. The external data source provides the bank with data on what other employers in the sector paid out as bonuses for the previous year. From the market data, the bank calculates the market average and benchmarks itself against it. At the end of each financial year, the bank conducts an assessment of its *actual* financial performance for the year against its agreed *targets* for the year. From this assessment, an overall bonus accrual figure is derived. If the division over-performs against its targets, then the overall bonus pot may be increased. But, if it under-performs, then it is reduced. Thus, although Ranjit's bonuses happened to increase significantly year-on-year, actually, there is no guarantee of a significant year-on-year increase in individuals' bonuses.

Once the bonus pots for the business areas are determined, they are given to the corresponding business area heads to divide and distribute to individuals working under them. The Human Resources department checks the allocations the heads make to individuals to ensure they are not tainted with any unlawful discrimination. It does this by reviewing the allocations by individuals' performance scores, genders, and ethnicities. The bonus allocations are checked for sensibility and reasonableness in terms of individuals' total remunerations, which is their base salary plus their bonus.

The bonus pot for the forthcoming 2007 bonus awards is anticipated to be the same size as the previous 2006 pot. The number of employees is more or less the same. Hence, I do not expect there to be any significant increases in people's bonus awards because any increases would have to be funded by reductions in other people's awards. For the Market Risk Department, specifically, I do not anticipate the forthcoming 2007 bonus awards will vary much from the previous year, subject to individuals' performances. If an individual performs poorly and receives an appraisal rating of 3/8, or lower, then the individual will not be entitled to a bonus award at all. This might free up some money to be paid to other individuals. I do not foresee there being significant increases in bonuses across the board. The support areas for the Financial Markets Division already possess the calibre of staff needed to function properly, meaning there are no areas where the bank is trying to attract significant numbers of staff. Nor is it at any risk of losing significant numbers of staff anywhere. The market pressure is not such that the bank needs to increase bonus payments significantly for the forthcoming 2007 awards. Ranjit's 2007 bonus award would not increase, if he were still employed at the bank.

The standard recruitment practice in the banking sector is for employers to compensate new employees for any accrued bonuses they might forgo by switching jobs. Also standard practice is for employers to pay out all deferred bonuses to employees upon their resignations.

'Yes,' she replies.

The respondents' counsel gives way to my counsel to cross-examine her.

'What do you know about Ranjit when the Director of the Financial Markets Division approaches you regarding his request for an opportunity to work on a voluntary basis?' my counsel asks.

'I was aware of the litigation,' she answers, 'but, knew nothing about the failure to comply with reinstatement orders. I knew he was employed at the bank, but I didn't know he was dismissed. I knew there is a claim for unfair dismissal and race discrimination, but didn't know what stage the claim is at'.

The chairman interjects, 'Mrs Rigsby, you say you were aware of the claim for unfair dismissal, but say you did not know he was dismissed. If you knew there is a claim for unfair dismissal, then it follows that you must have known he was dismissed'.

'Er,' she mumbles. Her face reddens. 'Yes, I did know he was dismissed,' she admits.

The chairman signals my counsel to continue.

'Do you know he is having difficulties in finding work when you advise the Director of Financial Markets?' my counsel asks.

'No, I didn't know that,' she answers.

'It might follow reasonably from a former employee's request to work on a voluntary basis,' my counsel says.

'I did wonder why he's making the request,' she replies, 'but, it didn't suggest to me he's having difficulties finding work. He didn't imply it in the wording of his request'.

'If the bank is inclined to help him, then it could try to address the security concerns you mention by taking some simple measures,' my counsel says, 'like, making some enquiries about him in its Market Risk Department where he worked. If such measures provide reliable assurance, then the bank could bind him with a confidentiality agreement'.

'He's not the only case refused,' she replies. 'The bank refuses everyone's requests. The bank does accommodate student interns for a fixed three-month period over the summer. But, it doesn't entertain requests for voluntary work from anyone else, not just from him'.

'Do you consider he might be a special case?' my counsel asks.

'No,' she answers.

'Moving on,' my counsel says. 'What do you mean by, *targets*, when you testify the bank conducts an assessment of its performance against targets for the purpose of setting a bonus pot?'

'I mean the budgeted financial profit & loss goals for the division,' she answers.

'You do not support your testimony with any specific evidence showing the budgeted goals,' my counsel says. 'Nor, do you evidence how the bank performed against them'.

'Er,' she mumbles. 'No, I don't'.

'Are economic market conditions reliable indicators of how the bank performs?' my counsel asks.

'No,' she answers.

'Does the bank award bonuses based on the prevailing market conditions?' my counsel asks.

'No,' she answers.

'Who decides the size of the bonus pot?' my counsel asks.

'Six people do,' she answers. 'They are: three members of the bank's Executive Committee; the Human Resources Rewards Director; the Chief Financial Controller; and me. The bank's Chief Executive Officer has overriding say on bonuses. The six of us decide the overall bonus pot for the entire bank and then, allocate it to the twelve divisions the bank consists of. The divisional heads decide how to distribute their pots to their staff. The process is protracted. It normally starts in October. It hasn't started yet for the forthcoming 2007 bonus awards. In November, the heads of business areas will be given an estimate of the size of the bonus pot they might receive for distribution to their staff. Then, in January, they'll be informed of the finalised amount'.

The chairman interjects, 'does that mean Mr Ong knows in January the size of the bonus pot he has for allocation?'

'Yes,' she answers.

The chairman signals my counsel to continue.

'You testify the Human Resources department checked the bonus allocations Mr Ong made to individuals for anomalies, unfairness, and unlawful discrimination,' my counsel says.

'That's correct,' she replies, 'and, I accept the tribunal found Ranjit's bonus award is tainted with race discrimination'.

'I have no more questions,' my counsel says.

The chairman invites the respondents' counsel to re-examine her witness. She declines. The chairman invites the judge on his right to cross-examine her.

'How many of the bank's employees does your role cover?' the judge asks.

'About two thousand,' she answers.

'Are prospective employers concerned by the fact that Mr Singh is dismissed from employment?' the judge asks.

'No,' she answers. 'The fact that he's dismissed is irrelevant to them. They care only whether or not he has the relevant skills and experience to perform their roles. I don't expect him to disclose that he litigated against his former employers. Redundancy is a completely acceptable answer. I recommend he explains his dismissal by redundancy'.

'I have no more questions,' the judge says.

The chairman invites the judge on his left to cross-examine her.

'Do employers use the services of a single recruitment agent exclusively, or of multiple agents?' the judge asks.

'Multiple,' she answers. 'The bank uses the services of ten agents. Agents tend not to talk to each other. So, it's quite normal for an employer to receive details of a particular candidate from a number of agents. We can receive details of a particular candidate from all ten of our agents'.

'Is it necessary for a job candidate to register with lots of agents?' the judge asks.

'No,' she answers, 'it's not necessary because employers usually give their vacancies to multiple agents. Registering with a few agents is enough for a candidate to cover the opportunities available on the market'.

'What do you make of Mr Singh registering with twenty-six agents?' the judge asks.

'From a fees and commissions perspective,' she replies, 'it isn't in an agent's best interest for a candidate to register with lots of agents. Registering with twenty-six agencies certainly isn't in the agencies' best interests at all, or in his. Twenty-six is far too many. He really shouldn't have registered with so many. He only lowered his chances of getting another job by registering with so many because he increases the competition between them. None of them will think he's worth investing much of their effort in. They'll leave him sitting on their backbench and concentrate their energies on their frontbench candidates, who they're more likely to realise returns on'.

'I have no more questions,' the judge says.

'What are the chances of Mr Singh earning again the same level of remuneration as he did in the Market Risk Controller role from which he is dismissed,' the chairman resumes.

'The chances are best if he can manage to get another job in market risk, his field of expertise and experience,' she answers.

'Are prospective employers concerned by the fact that

he is unemployed for almost one and a half years?' the chairman asks.

'Er,' she stalls. 'Not necessarily. The fact that he's unemployed means he's not tied into any notice period. Unlike employed candidates, he's available to start work immediately. This is a huge advantage he enjoys over employed candidates. Although he's been unemployed for a very long time now, it doesn't matter to employers as long as he can justify it properly. They won't look favourably, though, on someone who's spent such a long time applying for hundreds of jobs and not managed to get even one'.

7

ANGELA PAXTON'S TESTIMONY

~ Wednesday 22nd August 2007, 3:00 p.m. ~

'Mrs Paxton, is that your signature on the witness statement and is that the evidence you wish to give?' the respondents' counsel asks her, she having just sworn in at the witness stand.

She has presented the tribunal her statement regarding compensation. It says the following:

> The bank employs me as a Senior Human Resources Consultant. I coordinated the gathering of the statistical evidence on the respondents' behalf in relation to this reconvened remedy hearing. All of the statistical evidence is based on employees who resigned their employments at the bank voluntarily.
>
> At the time of his dismissal, Ranjit Singh was 39 years old and was a band C employee. The band C and D statistics show that 46% of the employees within those bands resigned their employments at the bank in 2006. The statistics for the age range *35 to 45* years show that 48% of employees within that age range resigned their employments at the bank in 2006. These statistics are based on the bank as a whole. They are not based specifically on its Financial Markets Risk Division, the division in which Ranjit was employed. Nevertheless, they clearly prove there is a high percentage of staff turnover within the bank in relation to staff of the same employee band and age range as Ranjit. The

statistical evidence in relation to the Financial Markets Risk Division, specifically, shows the portion of employees who resigned their employment is: 46% in 2003; 27% in 2004; 14% in 2005; and 36% in 2006. The statistical evidence clearly shows Ranjit would not remain in his employment at the bank for much longer, if he had not been dismissed.

I also provide a breakdown of the *average length of service* in years. The average length of service for an employee in the Financial Markets Risk area is 5 years. For a band C employee, it is 6 years. As Ranjit was employed at the bank since 2001, then, given the statistical evidence, I expect he would resign his employment sometime in 2006, the year in which he was dismissed. The statistical evidence reinforces that he would not remain in his employment at the bank much beyond his dismissal date.

I also provide evidence of staff turnover in the banking sector generally, so the rates of the bank may be compared with those of its competitors. The evidence I provide in this respect is based on information contained in the publically available Corporate Social Responsibility reports published by three UK financial institutions. The information shows the bank's staff turnover runs at a significantly higher rate than that of its three competitors. This also points to Ranjit not remaining in his employment at the bank much longer.

Neil Hobson has been headhunted by one of the bank's competitors. He has resigned his position and is working his notice of resignation. The Human Resources department informed me the decision not to replace him has been made because of the financial pressure on the Market

Risk Department. On his departure, the Market Risk Control team will continue to operate with one Controller and two Associates, and will report directly into Simon Ong.

As Ranjit was dismissed in April 2006, he worked four months of the 2006 bonus year. He is entitled to a bonus award for that portion of the year. The bank decided to calculate his bonus entitlement by taking the amount it awarded to Katia Mykonola, his peer, for the entire year and pro-rating it to the four months for which he was employed in the year. The bank paid the amount to him in March 2007.

Employers in the financial sector no longer make final salary pension schemes available to new employees. I note Ranjit intends to retrain as a secondary school mathematics teacher. As a teacher, he will be a member of the government's final salary pension scheme.

The bank provides support with its out-placement consultancy to all employees it makes redundant. The bank provided Ranjit with level B support. It consists of a ten-hour programme of support covering a range of job search skills, including: career assessment and analysis; and the launch of a job search campaign. The support is provided on a one-to-one basis with a professional out-placement consultant. If Ranjit took up the support, then the consultant assigned to him would be somebody who has the relevant skills and experience to be able to deal with someone of his level of seniority in the industry. The consultancy advised me Ranjit took up very little of the available support. He only engaged with the consultancy on 26th January 2006, when he completed the registration process allowing him access to the consultancy's website. On 1st

February, he used the consultancy's office facilities. On 14th February, he provided a copy of his CV for the consultants to review. I am advised he did not take up any face-to-face meetings with the professional consultants. The face-to-face meetings would have assisted him greatly in finding another job. He did not take up his full entitlement of support.

I provide a number of press releases from one of the recruitment agencies Ranjit is registered with. The press releases show the conditions of the job market in the City. The press release dated September 2006 clearly shows the job market is very buoyant. It includes an analysis of the number of jobs available against the number of candidates applying for them. It shows that from February to August 2006, there were 10,000 job vacancies on the market and only 8,000 available candidates. Clearly, the job market following his dismissal is characterised by significantly more vacancies than available candidates. I appreciate the press release does not relate specifically to risk vacancies or to risk professionals. Nevertheless, it shows the overall job market is buoyant. Given Ranjit's considerable experience and the buoyancy of the job market, I think it is highly odd he as not yet found another employment within the City.

I also provide a Financial Services Survey dated June 2007. It is conducted by CWP, one of the UK's largest accountancy firms. It shows confidence is increasing in relation to the financial sector. It shows financial institutions feel more positive about their positions. I believe the survey shows the general job market in the City is very buoyant and that Ranjit should have no problems in finding another job very quickly.

'Yes,' she replies.

The respondents' counsel gives way to my counsel to cross-examine her.

'Do you agree the more senior an employee is, the less likely he is to resign his employment at the bank?' my counsel asks.

'Potentially, that's so,' she answers. 'However, the Head of Market Risk Control stayed for only four years before resigning'.

'Neil Hobson, also a Head, remains over twelve years before deciding to resign,' my counsel says.

'Er, yes, that's correct,' she confirms.

'Individuals decide for themselves how long to stay,' my counsel says.

'Yes, that's correct,' she replies.

'You say the statistical evidence is based on employees who resigned,' my counsel says. 'Employees who retired are not included in the data set from which the statistics are computed'.

'That's correct,' she confirms.

'Nor are included employees who are made redundant, or who accept voluntary redundancy,' my counsel says.

'Correct,' she confirms.

'The statistics are based on people who resign voluntarily in order to take up employment elsewhere,' my counsel says.

'Hmm, yes,' she replies. 'Although, some of them might have left to do some travelling, and others because they encountered fortunate financial circumstances meaning they never need to work again'.

The chairman interjects, 'Mrs Paxton, what sorts of, *fortunate financial circumstances*, render individuals never needing to work again?'

'A lottery win,' she answers.

'Pray do tell how many of the leavers in the data set resigned because they won the lottery and never needed to work again,' the chairman says.

'Er, hmm,' she stalls. 'Probably none,' she answers in embarrassed tone.

'*Probably none*,' the chairman echoes her words, rolling his eyes.

Her face reddens. The chairman signals my counsel to continue.

'The statistics are based on people who resign to take up employment elsewhere,' my counsel continues.

'Er, yes, that's correct,' she confirms.

'Individuals who leave in order to travel tend to be younger than thirty-nine years,' my counsel says.

'Yes, that's correct,' she confirms.

'The statistics are based on people who have the security of their employment at the bank from which to search for other jobs to move to, at a time of their own choosing. They are in a strong position to move on their own terms,' my counsel says.

'That's correct,' she confirms. 'I imagine they'd try to negotiate better packages than they're on'.

'Individuals will not really consider moving unless they negotiate at least a twenty per cent improvement in their packages,' my counsel says.

'I don't know,' she replies. 'Twenty per cent seems a big increase to me. But, I admit investment banking isn't my area of expertise. I suppose some people might leave to take up employment that's less than ideal for some reasons'.

'If Ranjit were not dismissed, then the most *likely* reason he would leave at some subsequent point is to take up employment elsewhere,' my counsel says.

'Er, yes,' she replies. 'But, there's also the possibility he might be dismissed by a compulsory redundancy'.

'Are you aware of any pending redundancy situations that might result in his dismissal?' my counsel asks.

'No,' she answers. 'But, compulsory redundancy can't be ruled out in principle,' she adds.

'There are no redundancy situations pending that might

impact him,' my counsel says. 'Compulsory redundancy is ruled out in principle'.

'Er, hmm,' she mumbles.

'Is it reasonable to say,' my counsel continues, 'that an individual's bonus will increase, accordingly, as his base salary increases?'

'Yes,' she answers.

'Moving on to the out-placement support,' my counsel says. 'You suggest Ranjit does not take up any face-to-face meetings with a professional consultant'.

'That's correct,' she replies.

'But, the documentary evidence supplied to the tribunal contains two email correspondences between the out-placement consultancy and Ranjit, showing he attends two face-to-face consultation meetings with the consultants assigned to him, each of an hour's duration,' my counsel says. 'The fact is he attends two meetings'.

'I wasn't made aware of them,' she replies. 'I now accept he took up the face-to-face consultation service'.

'You also suggest he could use the services of the consultancy to a greater extent than he did,' my counsel says.

'That's correct,' she replies.

'The consultancy advises individuals according to their specific needs,' my counsel says.

'That's correct,' she replies.

'The consultancy is the expert, and is best placed to decide how much support each individual needs,' my counsel says.

'Er, yes, that's correct,' she confirms.

'If the consultants feel Ranjit's need is greater, then they would advise him to take up more of their support,' my counsel says.

'I should hope so,' she replies. 'But, I expected him to use up all of the support he was entitled to. If he did, he'd have managed to get another job a long time ago'.

'You are not privy to the discussions between them,'

my counsel says. 'The consultants are best positioned to advise him of the support he needs to take up'.

'Er, yes, correct,' she replies.

'Still, you suggest he should take up more support,' my counsel says.

'Er, hmm,' she mumbles.

'Moving on to the surveys and the press releases you reference,' my counsel continues. 'They provide very general information only, nothing specific at all to market risk roles or to market risk professionals'.

'That's correct,' she confirms.

'I have no more questions,' my counsel says.

The chairman invites the respondents' counsel to re-examine her witness. She declines.

The chairman invites the judge on his right to cross-examine her.

'Did Mr Singh resign his employment at the bank?' the judge asks her.

'No,' she answers. 'He was dismissed'.

'I have no more questions,' the judge says.

The chairman invites the judge on his left to cross-examine her.

'The evidence seems to suggest the longer an individual remains in the bank's employment, the less likely he is to resign,' the judge says.

'I disagree,' she replies.

'Putting the evidence aside, then,' the judge says, 'do *you* accept the longer someone stays, the less likely he is to resign?'

'Er, hmm,' she stalls. 'It depends on the role, I suppose. If the role is a short-term role, then the likelihood of resigning is high'.

'I have no more questions,' the judge says.

'Do you think length of service is relevant in Mr Singh's circumstances?' the chairman resumes.

'Yes, absolutely, I do,' she answers.

'The length of service figures you provide are based on

people who resigned to take up other employments,' the chairman says. 'They do not take into account employees who remain at the bank until their retirements'.

'Er, it's unrealistic to say people will work at the bank up to their retirement ages,' she replies.

'Surely, Mrs Paxton, such a large organisation that has existed for such a long time must have had some staff members who worked right up to their retirements,' the chairman puts to her.

'Er,' she stalls. 'Hmm, yes, I suppose it must have,' she concedes.

'Of course, it must have,' the chairman asserts. 'What is the average length of service for them?'

'Er, I don't know,' she answers.

8

RESPONDENTS' CASE

~ Thursday 23rd August 2007, 10:00 a.m. ~

'Mr Singh's only protest,' the respondents' counsel starts submitting the case against compensation to the tribunal, 'is that his and Miss Mykonola's redundancy scores, upon which the selection of the person to be dismissed is based, should be equal, but are unequal because unfairness and discrimination feature in the scoring exercise. If, hypothetically, unlawfulness did not feature, then their scores would be equal and a tiebreaker situation would come into play. Then, the person to be dismissed would be selected based on *attendance* records. Mr Singh was off work for a number of weeks, due to having suffered a leg break. His attendance is significantly poorer than Miss Mykonola's. This means he would certainly be selected for dismissal in the tiebreak and, consequently, be dismissed. On this basis, the evidence points unequivocally to the conclusion that he would be dismissed anyway, even if unlawfulness did not feature in the redundancy process. He is actually no worse off by experiencing unlawfulness; the outcome would be exactly the same. Consequently, he does not suffer any loss worthy of the legal remedy of compensation. No compensation is awardable to him in law. This is the respondents' primary submission on the case against compensation. In the circumstances, the tribunal must uphold this submission and not award any compensation, whatsoever. If the tribunal does not uphold this submission, then, and only then, do the respondents' following submissions become relevant. They concern how long Mr Singh would remain in their employment, if he were not dismissed, and whether he discharges his legal duty to mitigate his loss'.

'Starting with the matter of how long Mr Singh would remain in the respondents' employment,' she continues. 'First, the only wrong he suffers is the termination of his employment with the respondents. The tribunal cannot award compensation in excess of the loss of earnings inherent in his hypothetical continued employment with the respondents. Any losses of earnings inherent in hypothetical employments with subsequent employers are irrelevant in the legal remedy of compensation. Second, he would resign his employment with the respondents and leave entirely voluntarily within a very short time from the date of his dismissal. To say he would continue in the respondents' employment till his retirement age is implausible. A number of factors strongly suggest he would resign within just a few months from his dismissal date'.

'One factor,' she continues, 'is his attitude towards Mr Hobson, his line manager. The manner in which he relates to Mr Hobson indicates he cannot possibly continue in his employment for much longer. I accept Mr Hobson does not proffer any testimony towards this factor himself. I say the reason he does not is because he is a placid man. I invite the tribunal to conclude for itself that his character is so from his gentle responses in email correspondences to the very challenging language, and direct tone of address, Mr Singh subjects him to during the course of his employment. Other managers would find Mr Singh's language and manner of address intolerable. The stream of email correspondence tells a tale of disgruntlement and dissatisfaction on Mr Singh's part, particularly on the matter of the team's reporting line. His correspondences to Mr Hobson are loaded with coded criticisms and jibes at him. They evidence he has a withering contempt for Mr Hobson. The correspondences show he is not well seated and contented in his employment with the respondents. This is the true reason why he requested voluntary redundancy in 2004. All this shows he would not remain in his employment much longer'.

'Another factor,' she continues, 'is Mr Singh's expectation to rise up the corporate hierarchy. His expectation is clearly evidenced by his view that his career still has great capacity for progression. There are no vacancies higher up the ladder at the time of his dismissal. The prospect he faces by remaining in the respondents' employment is to remain at the level of a Market Risk Controller indefinitely. The only option he has for furthering his career is through employment at other organisations. He applies for the Head of Derivative Products Risk vacancy in his department, on the 27th of January 2006. The position is equivalent in seniority to Mr Hobson's role. The fact that he applies for it tells that he is eager to progress and would resign his current position at around this time'.

The chairman interjects, 'he applies for the vacancy after he is informed he is selected for dismissal. He applies for it in an attempt to save himself from being terminated. What is unknown to the tribunal is whether or not he would apply for it if he were not told he is selected for dismissal'.

'Hmm,' she contemplates.

'Also unknown,' the chairman continues, 'is whether or not his application for the role would succeed, if he were assessed properly and fairly in his last performance appraisal, instead of being criticised and underrated wrongfully'.

'The tribunal is able to deduce his application would fail,' she replies, 'because it knows Miss Mykonola also applies for the role and is unsuccessful'.

'Objection!' my counsel interjects. 'The tribunal has no such knowledge. Never before is any testimony, or other evidence to that effect, advanced and exposed to cross-examination'.

'Objection accepted,' the chairman says.

'Another factor,' the respondents' counsel resumes, 'is the fact that he takes up issue with Mr Ong's assessment of his 2003 mid-year performance. It evidences he is unsettled and unhappy in his employment, feeling he is not being credited properly for his achievements'.

'Moving on to the statistical evidence,' she says. 'The bank's staff turnover statistics evidence the time had arrived when Mr Singh would resign his employment and leave. The Head of Market Risk Control resigns after only four years of service. Mr Singh, having served four and a half years, is on the verge of resigning. His CV shows he changes employments, on average, every three years. He leaves his previous employer after a period of only six months, due to discomfort with its internal systems. This is very striking because it echoes precisely the sorts of themes of issues he is experiencing in the respondents' employment. He attends an interview at another financial institution in the early part of 2005. The evidence pointing to the conclusion that he is about to resign is overwhelming, particularly because he is so disgruntled with Mr Hobson'.

The chairman interjects, 'there is a world of difference between resigning and being dismissed suddenly. When a person resigns, say, to take up another employment, or to pursue other interests, then he does so voluntarily, under his own control, at a time of his own choosing. The situation he ends up in is of his own making. He suffers no loss caused by others. But, if he is dismissed suddenly, then the situation is forced on him. He may suffer some loss of earnings. All of the statistical evidence the respondents advance regarding their staff turnover is based on people who resign under their own control to take up other employments. Would Mr Singh resign *without* having another employment in place to move on to?'

'All indications are,' she answers, 'he would resign

within a matter of a few months. The reason for his resignation is irrelevant'.

'Hmm,' the chairman muses for a moment. Then, he signals her to continue.

'The manner in which Mr Singh expresses himself during the redundancy process is highly relevant,' she continues. 'It dovetails with the high degree of disgruntlement on his part and a mind-set of being reconciled to leaving his employment. He neither protests against being selected for dismissal, nor does he place any emphasis on the ways in which he may be saved from it. All he is interested in doing is posturing for a position from which he may gain an advantage in negotiating a financial settlement package from the respondents to tide him over for one or two years'.

'The press release from the recruitment agency he is registered with,' she continues, 'shows the job market is very buoyant at the time of his dismissal. Yet, at the same time, he suggests he needs between one to two years to recover from the dismissal. He suggests it only as a negotiation posture. It cannot reflect any knowledge or experience he has about the job market. Mr Marr, the respondents' Head of Trading Credit, testifies, *"the job market is really hot at the moment, especially in market risk roles"*. Mr Marr's testimony certainly dovetails with the press release. The tribunal must consider whether Mr Singh is trying to deceive it, or does his testimony reflect the true condition of the job market?'

She pauses momentarily to check the chairman for a reaction, and then resumes, 'turning now to his duty to mitigate his loss. Mr Singh does not equip himself adequately to conduct a proper job search. He does not avail himself of the full ten hours of out-placement support arranged for him. His testimony, that he attends two face-to-face meetings with the out-placement consultants, conflicts with the information Mrs Paxton receives. The fact is, he attends no such meetings and does not avail himself of the valuable support made available to him'.

'He claims,' she continues, 'being shunned by prospective employers for litigating against his former employers is the major impediment to his job search post the liability hearing. The impediment does not exist prior to the hearing. The tribunal must focus on the quality of his mitigation attempt in the period before the liability hearing. If he conducted a job search in a reasonable manner back then, then he would succeed in securing another job. Then, he would pre-empt facing the impediment and being unemployed for the longer time period of sixteen months. A number of factors give the impression he does not do much to assist himself in his job search back then. He uses the services of only three recruitment agents, compared to over twenty after the hearing. The tribunal must consider why he does not do so vice versa? The answer is because he does not take on the job search with maximum intensity and effort prior to the liability hearing. He holds back and stays his hand until various impediments came into play. When cross-examined about how much personal time he spends on applying for jobs prior to the liability hearing, he gives an evasive and obscure answer. He has to be pressed for a response on the matter. He only registers on the eFinanceJobs website in January 2007, after the liability hearing. He misses out on a whole year's worth of job opportunities on it. Why on earth does he not look at the website prior to the liability hearing, if he is serious about finding a job back then?'

'It is a well established legal principle,' she continues, 'that a wrongfully dismissed employee's duty to mitigate his loss is discharged if he acts as a reasonable person having no hope of receiving compensation would act. Mr Singh's effort to mitigate his loss during the period prior to the liability hearing is lacklustre. He carries out his duty with one eye on the prospect of compensation. Prior to the liability hearing, the reason he gives to recruitment agents and employers for his dismissal is redundancy. The reason is not detrimental to his career prospects. Post the liability hearing, the reasons he gives are, unfairness, discrimination, and the respondents' failure to comply with reinstatement orders. He gives these reasons knowing full well they will jeopardise his career prospects. The tribunal must focus on the crux of the difference in his behaviour after the liability hearing. The difference is due to a motive on his part to sabotage his employment prospects purposely, in order to collect financial compensation from the respondents. Any reasonable job candidate, including Mr Singh, would understand volunteering information about litigation is highly likely to damage career prospects. This provides a compelling explanation for why a number of promising job opportunities, post the liability hearing, appear to be scuppered'.

'Any notion,' she continues, 'that he is motivated by a selfless desire to display absolute candour to agents and employers by setting out the entire picture, regardless of self-detriment, is incorrect because he is not absolutely frank and open to them in the period prior to the liability hearing. Back then, he keeps hidden from them that a liability hearing is pending. They have a right and a direct interest in knowing. Litigation will take up significant amounts of his time and energy. He will be distracted significantly from his employment responsibilities to them and risk publicity, all of which will impact them directly'.

The chairman interjects, 'although a liability hearing is pending at the time, he cannot possibly know where the process is going to end up. Your argument requires the tribunal to assume he knows with absolute certainty that the pending hearing will occur. The assumption is unreasonable. He cannot possibly know for certain. There are all sorts of factors in reality that can bring the process of litigation to a conclusion ahead of any pending hearing. To say he lack candour is extremely harsh'.

'Harsh, but true,' she asserts.

'Hmm,' the chairman muses. Then, he signals her to continue.

'He knows the explanation he proffers after the liability hearing is detrimental to his career prospects,' she continues. 'If he wishes, then he could instead say, he was dismissed *in connection with redundancy*. This is a wholly innocuous alternative explanation. He acts unreasonably in his duty to mitigate his loss by continuing to proffer the detrimental explanation'.

'He suffers no loss worthy of the legal remedy of compensation,' she continues. 'If there were any such loss, which there is not, then the loss would run only up to the hypothetical date at which he would leave the respondents' employment, for whatever reasons, whether voluntarily or otherwise. Limiting damage to the loss of earnings inherent in an employee's hypothetical continued employment with his *existing* employer is the conventional approach commended by legal precedents. Any losses the employee might continue to suffer in hypothetical employments with *subsequent* employers cannot be included in the legal remedy of compensation'.

'His evidence on mitigation prior to the liability hearing,' she continues, 'demonstrates a mere trickle of an effort to find another job. The hard fact is he registers with only three recruitment agencies, which together manage to produce only ten leads for jobs in an entire year. To suggest he discharges his duty with just one lead per month is absurd. Post the liability hearing, by which time he is unemployed for a whole year and the issue of being shunned by employers becomes relevant, his mitigation activity goes mad with applications for a hundred and twelve jobs. He admits he needs to be energetic and visible on the job market. Prior to the liability hearing, he is neither energetic, nor visible. He becomes so only after the liability hearing, when he finally starts looking at the eFinanceJobs website and registers with more recruitment agents. But he goes too far, registering with over twenty agents. Mrs Rigsby testifies that he reduces his chances of getting a job by acting against the agents' interests, by registering with so many and increasing the competition between them. He does this purposely with one eye on the prospect of compensation, knowing full well it will reduce his career prospects'.

'He testifies that he discloses the reasons for his departure from his employment with the respondents on a need-to-know basis only,' she continues. 'However, the email correspondence with agents clearly shows the contrary, that he discloses the reasons prior to them being elicited from him'.

The chairman interjects, 'he feels obliged to disclose the reasons to them by the terms and conditions he signs up to when registering with them'.

'My point is still valid,' she rebuts, 'because he discloses more information than is necessary. He unnecessarily volunteers his bonus is tainted with race discrimination, and that the respondents failed to comply with the reinstatement orders. The tribunal must ask itself why he volunteers details in excess of needs? The answer is, because he wants to give prominence to the issues'.

'Hmm,' the chairman muses for a moment. Then, he instructs her to continue.

'Moving on to the matter of who is to blame for his dismissal,' she says. 'He himself is to blame. He brings the dismissal upon himself by showing a low level of respect for Mr Hobson, his line manager, throughout the course of his employment. The stream of email correspondences from him to Mr Hobson shows his conduct towards Mr Hobson is *highly hostile*, *ill judged*, *perverse*, *foolish*, and *bloody-minded*. The conduct feeds into Mr Hobson's assessment of him, and contributes to his dismissal. Mr Hobson's unfairness towards him is simply the other side of the coin of his appalling conduct towards

Mr Hobson. Mr Singh is the only one culpable for any loss he might suffer. In the analysis of compensation, the tribunal must diminish his loss completely to zero, to reflect that he brings the dismissal upon his own head'.

The chairman interjects, 'wronged employees rarely seek reinstatement, and tribunals even more rarely order it. But, Mr Singh sought it, and the tribunal ordered it. The tribunal cannot recall any employer ever before failing to comply with reinstatement orders. The respondents failed. If Mr Singh were reinstated, then, effectively, there would be no dismissal. He would be back in his employment, as though nothing had happened. How does the respondents' failure to comply with the reinstatement orders fit in with their argument that Mr Singh is to blame for his own dismissal?'

'The respondents' failure to comply with the reinstatement orders is completely irrelevant in the remedy of compensation,' she answers as a matter of fact. 'The tribunal simply must reduce his loss to zero to reflect that he is culpable for his own dismissal, and, accordingly, not award any compensation'.

'Hmm,' the chairman contemplates. Then, he signals her to continue.

'Moving on to address the matter of the respondents' failures to follow the statutory redundancy procedures,' she says, 'which entitle the tribunal to uplift by ten per cent to fifty per cent any compensation award it might make. The respondents humbly request the tribunal to show them leniency, and apply an uplift of the minimum level of ten per cent only. Their failures are not committed deliberately, but are the results of inadvertent oversights'.

The chairman interjects, 'the circumstances of an offending employer are relevant in deciding the level at which to set the uplift. If an employer is large, established, retains professionals with employment subject matter expertise, and chooses deliberately not to comply with the procedures, then the uplift ought to be set at the maximum level of fifty per cent. If, on the other hand, the employer is small, poorly resourced, and is inexperienced and naïve in employment matters, then the uplift ought to be set towards the lower end of the range. The respondents are experienced employers with in-house professional Legal and Human Resources departments. They are familiar with the procedures. It seems they just do not bother to comply with them. In the circumstances, the uplift ought rightly to be set towards the top end of the range'.

'Although the respondents fail substantially,' she replies, 'they do not fail completely. They do comply with some of the procedures'.

9

CLAIMANT'S CASE

~ Thursday 23rd August 2007, 11:00 a.m. ~

'The facts are as follows,' my counsel starts submitting my case on compensation to the tribunal. 'Mr Singh is a professional working in a specialist and niche area. He is fairly senior in terms of age and experience. He is a substantial way up the corporate hierarchy at the bank. Most of the vacancies on the job market are for roles that are junior compared to the one he is dismissed from. The sorts of roles he is suited to rarely come on to the external job market. The reason is because employers, including the respondent bank, prefer to promote internal candidates into them, rather than recruit external ones'.

'Following the respondents' failure to comply with the tribunal's reinstatement orders,' she continues, 'Mr Singh finds himself in a predicament. When prospective employers ask him why he left his employment, he feels constrained to answer truthfully. They almost always ask him why he left? Although he cannot know for certain, the pattern of events he experiences leads him to believe prospective employers shun him for litigating against his former employers. The respondents acknowledge that prospective employers victimise him for litigating against them, and that his job search is handicapped as a result. They acknowledge it by the questions and the constructs they put to him under cross-examination, and by the arguments they submit in their case against compensation. Not only do they *acknowledge* it, but also they *demonstrate* it themselves by their initial reason for refusing reinstatement, that is, because he litigated against them.

Their failure to reinstate him deals him a severe blow. It burdens him with a crippling disadvantage on the job market'.

'He begins his job search initially in the field of market risk,' she continues. 'As time goes by, he spreads his search further afield, to product control, valuation control, auditing, and other areas. He does not find a job. There are no jobs opportunities pending. Eventually, he reaches out even further, to teaching. He will embark on a teaching career in a few days time. If a job suddenly turns up over the next few days, then, of course, he will take it. The overwhelming likelihood is his career in banking is over. Once he embarks on the teacher-training course, its intense and demanding workload will diminish his ability to search for employment back in the financial sector. Realistically, he is not going to be able to get another job comparable with the one he is dismissed from'.

'At the remedy hearing, on the 3rd of January 2007,' she continues, 'the respondents openly criticise him for not registering with more recruitment agents than he does. They criticise him for not making use of the eFinanceJobs website. There will always be steps the respondents can point to that he could take in his job search because it is impossible for him, as it also is for anyone else, to be exhaustive and take absolutely every step. Just because the respondents can point to steps that he does not take, it does not mean the steps he takes are unreasonable or inadequate. The correct test to apply is not whether he takes every possible step, but whether the steps he takes amount to reasonableness on his part'.

'Turning to the matter of disclosing to prospective employers the circumstances of his departure from the respondents' employment,' she says. 'His legal duty to mitigate his loss cannot override his duty *not to mislead society*. The test of reasonableness must be conducted with this principle in mind. There cannot be a positive duty on him to mislead employers in order to protect the respondents from the consequences of their own wrongdoings. The law cannot possibly be right to require him to mislead employers in order to mitigate his loss, even if he thinks they will victimise him when he tells them the truth'.

'Turning to the respondents' suggestion that, if Mr Singh does not have the prospect of compensation before him, then he would not explain his departure with unfairness, discrimination, and the failure to comply with reinstatement orders,' she continues. 'The explanations he gives should be looked at in the context of his duty to be honest. He is of the integrity that he would not behave any differently even if the prospect of compensation is not before him'.

'The respondents argue he could, instead, say he is dismissed, *"in connection with redundancy",*' she continues. 'If he says this, then any diligent interviewer will follow up with further questions drilling down into exactly what he means by, *"in connection with redundancy"*. They will not leave it alone. They will extract the full details from of him. In his line of work, maintaining employers' trust is absolutely critical. Answering questions evasively, obscurely, or falsely during the recruitment process is counterproductive to maintaining their trust. It could get him into serious trouble and highly stressful situations further down the line'.

The chairman interjects, 'do you mean he would be making misrepresentations?'

'Yes,' she answers.

'Hmm,' the chairman muses for a moment. Then, he signals her to continue.

'At the initial remedy hearing, on the 3rd of January,' she continues, 'he gives a clear testimony of his attempt at mitigation. He answers all of the questions put to him under cross-examination without giving any evasive or obscure responses. His testimony at the time includes the account that he uses the services of three specialist recruitment agents. It also includes the explanation that looking at the eFinanceJobs website is not mandatory because it merely connects candidates with recruitment agents. In the period prior to the liability hearing, he does not deploy a *scattergun* approach in his job search. He targets job opportunities more accurately; applying for vacancies that are more closely matched with his profile, vacancies he stands a greater chance of getting. The respondents criticise him severely for not deploying a scattergun approach. They criticise him for not using the services of more agents, and for not using the eFinanceJobs website. The fact that he does not manage to get another job by a targeted approach does not, of itself, mean his attempt at mitigation is unreasonable. His job search prior to the liability hearing is entirely reasonable, even though it does not yield many interviews and certainly no job offers. Miss Mykonola, when made redundant from her previous job, is unemployed for a period of eighteen months before eventually securing a job with the respondents. Such is the nature of the job search at their level, in their profession'.

'After the liability hearing,' she continues, 'he deploys a scattergun approach in order to address the respondents' criticisms of him. Even then, he does not manage to get another job. It is shallow to say his acts of registering with more agents, and registering on the eFinanceJobs website, demonstrate his mitigation attempt prior to the liability hearing is unreasonable. Employers use the services of multiple agents to reach the candidates available on the external job market. Mrs Rigsby testifies to the effect that it is sufficient for him to register with just a few agents in order to gain exposure to most of the available vacancies. Registering with lots of agents is unnecessary, and can be counterproductive in that it can reduce his credibility. She also testifies to the effect that registering with lots of agents will put them off for commercial reasons relating to commissions and fees. When he deploys a targeted approach, the respondents say he should deploy a scattergun approach. When he does as they say and deploys a scattergun approach, then they say he should deploy a targeted approach. They cannot have it both ways. Just because he changes his job search strategy after the liability hearing, to apply also for many vacancies that he believes are too junior for him, it does not mean his former strategy prior to the liability hearing, of applying mainly for vacancies that more closely match his profile, is inadequate. He only implements the change in order to address the criticisms the respondents make of his former strategy, not because he believes his strategy is inadequate'.

'Each time he applies to the respondents for a vacancy that is too junior for him,' she continues, 'they screen him out immediately. Of course, they would do; he is too senior for the roles and will imbalance their workplace environment'.

'The respondents suggest he should cast his net wider,' she continues. 'He does exactly that. Still, no job emerges, no matter how wide he casts the net. In the end, he has to acknowledge he cannot remain unemployed indefinitely, and that he needs to consider a career change. A change to teaching is a reasonable step for him to take after sixteen months of unemployment'.

'He acts reasonably in attempting to mitigate his loss,' she continues. 'He is entitled to be compensated for the loss he suffers. The loss he suffers is the difference between the amount he *would* earn, if he were not dismissed, and the amount he *will* earn in teaching'.

'Moving on to address the respondents' submission that they would dismiss him quite fairly and lawfully anyway, if they had not dismissed him unlawfully,' she continues. 'A retrospective hypothetical consideration of what might have happened under fair conditions is not permitted when unlawful discrimination features in a dismissal. Then, what *might* have happened is irrelevant. The correct approach is to consider what *actually* happened, and whether the unlawful discrimination contributes materially to the loss suffered. If it does, then he is entitled to be compensated for the entire damages he suffers'.

'Furthermore,' she continues, 'the respondents' submission depends on there being a genuine and bona fide redundancy situation, which is not the case here, according to the facts the tribunal determined on liability. On liability, Mr Singh submitted the case that Mr Hobson targets him for dismissal. Then, when there arises a need to cut costs in the department, but not necessarily by reduced headcount, he approaches Mr Ong, the Director of the department, and volunteers to make a Market Risk Controller redundant. Only one employee out of the seventy in the entire area is made redundant, that is, Mr Singh. The redundancy is not the outcome of a *genuine* redundancy situation. It is the outcome of a *sham* redundancy exercise that Mr Hobson creates with the exclusive purpose of dismissing Mr Singh, specifically. If Mr Hobson did not target Mr Singh to start with, then he would not volunteer to make a Controller redundant, and there would not be any redundancy exercise in the department. Then, nobody would be dismissed'.

'The tribunal simply does not know what would happen if Mr Hobson did not target Mr Singh,' she continues. 'It does not know whether the desired cost reduction would be achieved by other means, besides a headcount reduction'.

The chairman interjects, 'I recall Mr Ong testifying that his main expenditure is on salaries and bonuses. Therefore, the cost reduction would have to be achieved by reduced headcount through compulsory redundancies'.

'That is not necessarily the conclusion to be logically drawn,' she replies. 'He also testifies that he loses headcount naturally through resignations and does not always need to replace everyone who leaves, because, sometimes, resignations provide him with the opportunity to re-organise work more efficiently. This signifies a high chance that the desired cost reduction would be achieved without any compulsory redundancies'.

'If the desired cost saving *is* to be achieved through compulsory redundancies,' the chairman says, 'then what is the chance that Mr Singh would be dismissed?'

'There is no way to know for certain in which of the teams the headcount reductions would occur,' she answers. 'The entire area consists of seventy employees. Only one employee, Mr Singh, is made redundant. Assuming everyone has the same chance of dismissal, then the mathematical probability that Mr Singh will be dismissed is *one out of seventy*. That is less than a one and a half per cent chance. This means there is over a ninety-eight and a half per cent chance that he will not be dismissed. To adjust his loss by an amount as small as one and a half per cent hardly seems worth the bother'.

'The evidence,' she continues, 'particularly of the natural rate of staff attrition by resignations, and of the millions of pounds of wholly discretionary bonuses the bank is able to afford to pay to employees, does not point to a pressure to achieve cost reductions through compulsory redundancies. Coupled with the fact that nobody else out of the other sixty-nine employees is made redundant, this all suggests the most natural and likely conclusion to be drawn is that nobody at all would be made redundant in order to achieve the desired cost saving. The situation is not one where there would be redundancies. The reason there is the one redundancy is because Mr Hobson exploits the redundancy procedures to achieve what he personally sets out to do, that is, to dismiss Mr Singh'.

'Hmm,' the chairman contemplates. 'Do continue,' he says.

'Moving on to address the respondents' submission that Mr Singh would resign his employment within a matter of a few months anyway, if they did not dismiss him,' she says. 'The tribunal has observed and experienced Mr Singh directly for itself here at the hearings. It has probed and examined him. It has seen that he performs his role at the bank energetically, assiduously, and impressively. It has seen that he knows his job to the best of anyone's ability and is very good at it. These are not the characteristics of someone who is so disgruntled or discontented that he is on the verge of resigning. He has absolutely no intention of resigning. This is very clearly evidenced by the fact that he refuses Mr Hobson's offer of voluntary redundancy. Mr Hobson makes the offer in November 2005, before he proceeds to dismiss him compulsorily. If Mr Singh wished to leave, then he could very easily negotiate a package with Mr Hobson under his offer. He refuses Mr Hobson plainly and clearly. He wants to remain. Then, when he is notified he is selected for dismissal, he fights vigorously to avoid being dismissed. He challenges his year-end performance appraisal. He engages in the so-called consultation process and raises objections to being selected for dismissal. He proposes suggestions to avoid being dismissed. He raises formal grievances and appeals. Finally, here at the tribunal, he seeks reinstatement over and above compensation. All this points unequivocally to the conclusion that he wants to remain in his employment'.

'Moving on to the statistical evidence the respondents provide regarding its staff turnover rates,' she continues. 'The statistics relate to employees who *resign* their employments to take up employments elsewhere. Mr Singh does not resign to take up another employment. He is forced out, twice, effectively. First, by the unlawful dismissal, which hurls him into unemployment. Then again, by the respondents' failure to comply with the reinstatement orders, which leaves him on the job market with the disadvantage of the stigma associated with having litigated against his former employers. He is entitled to be compensated for the disadvantage he suffers on the job market because it arises and flows directly out of the respondents' conduct. But for the unlawful dismissal and the failure to comply with reinstatement orders, Mr Singh would continue in the respondents' employment until he resigns to take up better-paid employment elsewhere, or until he reaches his retirement age. He certainly would not leave to put himself in the disadvantageous position the respondents have put him in, of having no job and looking for another one from an unemployed status, and having litigated against his former employers'.

'Moving on to address the respondents' submission that Mr Singh brings the dismissal upon his own head by behaving in a hostile and disrespectful manner towards Mr Hobson,' she says. 'He acts in no such way. He does not contribute in any way whatsoever to the dismissal falling on his head. The tribunal investigated the matter of his conduct towards Mr Hobson during the course of his employment. It also witnessed for itself his manners towards Mr Hobson here at the tribunal hearings. The tribunal would not order reinstatement if it found he contributed in any way at all to his own dismissal, or harbours any ill will towards Mr Hobson. The respondents' argument is pre-empted by the fact that the tribunal ordered reinstatement and ruled the respondents failed to comply with the orders. Never, before the legal remedy of reinstatement coming into play, does Mr Hobson say or record anywhere that Mr Singh treats him with disrespect or hostility, despite having ample opportunity to do so. He could have recorded it during the course of Mr Singh's employment, in his mid-year and year-end formal appraisals. He could have said so in the bank's investigations of the grievances and appeals Mr Singh lodged. He could have said it in his testimony during the liability hearing. Only after the legal remedy of reinstatement coming into play does he start to deploy the *tactic* of testifying that Mr Singh disrespects him. He does this because he does not want Mr Singh reinstated. The tactful nature of his testimony, and the absence of any contemporaneous evidence supporting it, evidences that Mr Singh does not treat him with disrespect'.

'Clearly, Mr Singh is not culpable for his own dismissal,' she continues, 'not even to the slightest bit. The loss he suffers should not be reduced, whatsoever, in the calculation of compensation'.

'The respondents begin the matter of remedy,' she continues, 'by rejecting outright Mr Singh's request for reinstatement on the unlawful basis that he litigated against them. They begin with a robust conviction that they will not countenance his reinstatement, come what may. They close their minds completely to the matter. They do not even consider it properly. Although their reasoning changes in due course from an unlawful basis to a lawful one, their approach continues essentially to remain to be one of not countenancing his reinstatement because he litigated against them. By their failure to comply with the reinstatement orders, they deny Mr Singh the best opportunity he has to mitigate his loss. If they comply with the orders, then his mitigation difficulties disappear, because he will not be on the job market. The stigma associated with having litigated against his former employers, and the other three factors that disadvantage him severely in finding another job, will not come into play, if the respondents comply with the reinstatement orders. The effect of the respondents' conduct is not only to deny Mr Singh his career with themselves, but also to deny him his career elsewhere'.

'Moving on to address the respondents' failures to comply with the statutory redundancy procedures,' she continues. 'Although the respondents do not fail completely in their duty to comply, they do fail to a huge degree. The purpose of the statutory procedures is to protect employees from their employers. By failing to apply the procedures, the respondents deny Mr Singh the protection society intends to afford him. The bank is a large, established employer, with dedicated Legal and Human Resources departments staffed with professionals who know the procedures expertly. It has no excuse for failing to apply them. It simply does not bother to apply them. The uplift ought to be set towards the top end of the permitted ten per cent to fifty per cent range'.

'Turning now to address the matter of the unnecessary distress the respondents cause Mr Singh,' she continues. 'Mr Hobson records on Mr Singh's official employment record negative remarks that will give prospective employers cause for grave concerns about him. The remarks will feed into references for employments the bank provides to employers. The references will preclude employers from recruiting him. Mr Hobson's official remarks jeopardise his career. They are a considerable source of intense mental distress for Mr Singh because they are completely unfounded, are made irresponsibly, and are of critical significance to his livelihood. Never before the redundancy exercise coming into play, does Mr Hobson make any such criticisms of him, despite having ample opportunity to do so. The bank's officers responsible for judging the formal grievances and appeals that Mr Singh lodges, and its various HR department representatives who assisted them, all engage in a process of denial and towing the party line. They do not take the issues seriously. They do not take seriously the input Mr Singh gives to try to resolve them amicably and privately. They do not conduct their investigations properly. Mr Singh experiences *institutional denial*. Then, the respondents contest the allegations of unfairness and race discrimination vigorously. Upon being found guilty of each and every allegation against them, even by a unanimous tribunal, they express no form of apology and show no remorse for their conduct. A decision by them to reinstate Mr Singh would assuage the considerable distress they cause him. Instead, they resist reinstatement vigorously with a highly *malicious* and *unnecessary* attack on his character, by which they cause even more distress. Then, on failing to comply with the reinstatement orders, when compliance is perfectly possible, they appear not to be able to care less for their failure. They do not express any apology or remorse for it, or for the detrimental consequences it entails for Mr Singh'.

10

JUDGEMENT DAY

~ Friday 24th August 2007, 2:00 p.m. ~

Preparing mentally for the worst while hoping for the best is what I've spent the past twenty-four hours doing, over which the tribunal deliberated its decision on compensation behind closed doors. The risk analyst in me cannot help but want to try to forecast the tribunal's likely decision. My counsel's remarks, the average compensation award is only nine thousand pounds and the tribunal will find it difficult to deviate far north of that, are inputs that weigh heavily in the analysis. The fact that the tribunal has vast freedom to exercise discretion in the deliberation of compensation, a matter entailing considerable uncertainty and allowing for much subjectivity, will act against me. It pains me to think of the probable outcome; I shut my eyes, but it is impossible to shut my mind to it.

We are all gathered before the tribunal to receive its decision. The public gallery is full with spectators. I sit in my regular spot, in the public gallery immediately behind my counsel and her assistant, on the far right hand side of the courtroom. Neil, Simon, Veronica, and the bank's officers sit together in their usual spot, in the public gallery immediately behind their counsel and her assistant, on the far left hand side of the room. The thought pains me that they deprive me of reinstatement, a remedy so replete with mutual benefits and so desirable on so many levels. It vexes me that we need not be here right now, but for their belligerent compliance failure.

'All stand,' the courtroom attendant cries out.

We rise to our feet. The three judges emerge from

their chamber's door in the wall behind the platform with the judges' bench at the head of the room. They file in, take up their seats, and gaze down authoritatively on their courtroom.

'Be seated,' the attendant cries out.

My nerves run high. I brace myself to receive the tribunal's decision.

'At the end of the liability hearing on the 15th of December 2006,' the chairman begins, 'the tribunal upheld the allegations of unfair dismissal and race discrimination that Mr Singh brought against the respondents. Then, at the start of the remedy hearing on the same day, he requested reinstatement, which the tribunal subsequently ordered. Then, on the 3rd of January 2007, the tribunal found the respondents failed to comply with the reinstatement orders. On the same day, the tribunal heard evidence concerning mitigation from Mr Singh and Mr Hobson. The hearing was adjourned due to lack of available time to complete the legal process. The hearing reconvened three days ago, on the 21st of August. The tribunal heard evidence concerning mitigation during the eight-month adjournment period. It also received over a thousand pages of additional documentary evidence in relation to mitigation and compensation'.

'If the respondents did not dismiss Mr Singh,' the chairman continues, 'then he would consider positions equivalent in seniority to Mr Hobson's. Since his dismissal, he applies for over one hundred and twenty-three jobs that he is able to evidence with documentation, but is considered for others too, which he cannot evidence with documentation because of the informal nature of the recruitment processes regarding them. He applies for a diverse range of jobs in the financial sector, spanning a variety of disciplines and fields. He does not confine his job search to market risk, the discipline in which he worked for the preceding nine years and possesses specific expertise in'.

'Four job applications,' the chairman continues, 'are to the respondent bank for vacancies it advertised on its website. One is the Market Risk Associate vacancy in the Market Risk Control team, being a subordinate role to the Market Risk Controller role from which he is dismissed. The respondents reject his application on the basis that his experience and skills are far in excess of their requirements for the position. In relation to his application for the Equity Dealer vacancy, only after he chases for a response does the bank eventually, after three months, inform him it has filled the vacancy. Regarding his application for the Model Validation Analyst vacancy, he chases the bank repeatedly for a response. Eventually, after four months, the bank responds informing him it is unable to proceed with his application because the vacancy is put on hold due to business requirements. Regarding his application for the Auditor vacancy, other than requesting his CV, the bank never responds to him, or progresses his application'.

'He approaches a number of the bank's departments in May 2007,' the chairman continues, 'with requests to work for them on a voluntary basis. He takes the initiative in order to increase his chances of finding another employment elsewhere, based on his belief that prospective employers will look on it positively. The bank rejects all of his requests on the basis that it does not generally entertain voluntary work'.

'He believes,' the chairman continues, 'the respondents' failure to comply with the reinstatement orders brings into play four factors that severely damage his ability to find another job on the job market. The factors are: the stigma associated with litigating against his former employers; the issues surrounding his departure; the long period of time for which he is unemployed; and the fact that he does not leave his career in market risk voluntarily, and tries to return to it through reinstatement'.

'So far as the matter of stigma of litigating against his former employers is concerned,' the chairman continues,

'Mr Singh draws attention to the fact that the respondents initially refuse his request for reinstatement on the unlawful basis that he litigated against them. He categorises their subsequent act, of superseding their initial reason with an alternative lawful one, as an act of fronting their genuine, unlawful motive with a disingenuous, lawful one. He believes in many situations where employers decided to reject his job applications, the reasons they gave were disingenuous fronts for their genuine reason, being that he litigated against his former employers. He supports his belief by reference to at least four prospective employers who seem not to pursue his applications by reason of stigma, and by reference to a recruitment agent, who shuns him after he discloses the reasons for his departure from his job'.

'Following the tribunal's judgement on liability,' the chairman continues, 'Mr Singh decides to inform recruitment agents the reasons for his departure are: unfairness; race discrimination; and the respondents' failure to comply with reinstatement orders. He also decides to provide these same reasons to prospective employers when they ask him why he left his job with the respondents? The respondents subject him to severe criticism for doing this, claiming he unnecessarily volunteers the reasons. They suggest he could instead say he was dismissed, *"in connection with redundancy"*.

'The tribunal finds Mr Singh does not volunteer the reasons for his departure to prospective employers,' the chairman rules. 'Only when questioned directly on the matter of his departure does he then give the reasons. He is asked virtually in every interview why he left his job? When asked, he answers'.

'In virtually every interview,' the chairman continues, 'he is also asked why he is unemployed for such a long time? This is a matter of concern to employers and affects his job search adversely'.

'When he tries to get jobs outside of the field of market

risk,' the chairman continues, 'he finds justifying he is pursuing them because of a genuine desire from within is very difficult, in the light of the fact that he did not leave his career in market risk voluntarily and tried to return to it through reinstatement'.

'His experience,' the chairman continues, 'is that employers mostly fill vacancies suitable for him by promoting internal candidates, rather than by recruiting candidates from the external job market. In these circumstances, he finds he has to pursue junior vacancies to try to get back into employment and then, work back up the levels of seniority. He gives evidence that the respondents themselves practise internal promotion over external recruitment'.

'His level of experience and qualifications are such,' the chairman continues, 'that the normal route into employment is via recruitment agents. He describes agents as being the main sources of vacancies and as gatekeepers to the job opportunities. The respondents criticise him severely for not making use of a particular website in his job search, namely, eFinanceJobs. When he uses it, he finds the opportunities on it mirror those being provided to him by the recruitment agents he is registered with. On a significant number of occasions, he is approached for the same vacancy by a number of agents. In the period before the liability hearing, he uses a handful of agents only. At the initial remedy hearing in January, the respondents criticise him severely for not using more. During the adjournment period of the remedy hearing, he reacts to their criticisms by increasing the number of agents to twenty-six. The respondents then subject him to severe criticism that he uses too many'.

'Regarding the extent to which he avails himself of the support from the out-placement consultancy the respondents arranged for him,' the chairman continues. 'He attends two one-hour, face-to-face consultancy sessions with the out-placement consultants. He does not take up any more time because the consultants advise him he is pursuing his job search appropriately. The tribunal rejects the respondents' suggestion that he does not take up *any* of the support they arranged for him'.

'Regarding the evidence Mrs Paxton puts forward on the respondents' behalf in relation to the job market generally in the financial sector,' the chairman continues. '*General* evidence is of little material assistance to the tribunal in reaching conclusions on the *specific* issues it has to decide on'.

'Turning now,' the chairman continues, 'to the matter of whether Mr Singh would be dismissed, if he were not subjected to unfair and discriminatory treatments. What *might* happen hypothetically under fair conditions is relevant in the remedy of compensation if, and only if, discrimination does *not* feature in the dismissal. The fact that Mr Singh suffers discrimination renders irrelevant the consideration of the hypothetical outcomes. In the circumstances, the correct approach in performing the analysis of compensation is to consider whether the discrimination he suffers makes a *material* contribution to the loss he sustains. On the basis of the tribunal's findings at the end of the liability hearing, there is no doubt whatsoever the discrimination he is subjected to contributes materially to the loss he suffers. From this perspective, he is entitled to recover his loss in full'.

'Moving on now to the matter of how long Mr Singh would remain in the respondents employment, if he were not dismissed,' the chairman continues.

'Starting with the respondents' submission that he has a highly unsatisfactory relationship with Mr Hobson, his line manager,' the chairman says. 'First, the tribunal notes Mr Singh is willing to be reinstated under Mr Hobson. It also notes his willingness is genuine, which it could not be if he has an unsatisfactory relationship with him. It is Mr Hobson who is not prepared to countenance Mr Singh's reinstatement under himself. Second, Mrs Paxton testifies that Mr Hobson is leaving the bank's employment soon, in order to take up employment at another financial institution. His time as Mr Singh's line manager, and the relationship between them, would end now. In the circumstances, and in any event, the relationship is not a factor that supports the respondents' claim that Mr Singh would resign soon'.

'Moving on to the respondents' submission that Mr Singh is unsettled and unhappy in his employment because he takes up issues with Mr Ong's assessment of his 2003 mid-year performance,' the chairman says. 'Although Mr Ong marks him down, he is not marked down in prior appraisals, nor subsequent ones. To focus just on the 2003 mid-year appraisal, in isolation of the other appraisals, is artificial and misleading. The matter of the 2003 mid-year appraisal does not support the respondents' submission that Mr Singh would resign soon'.

'Regarding the statistics Mrs Paxton sets out on behalf of the respondents in regards to how long Mr Singh would remain in their employment,' the chairman says. 'The statistics are very general. They indicate there are some individuals who leave the bank's employment after a short period of years to take up employments at other employers. The tribunal is unable to extrapolate, from their very general nature, any more significant meaning than there is some chance that Mr Singh would leave the respondents' employment at some stage. The tribunal concludes no more from them than what Mr Singh submits, that is, if he resigns, then it would not be to put himself in a position where he would be without the security afforded by another employment. On the balance of probabilities, the tribunal concludes the only circumstance in which he would leave is to take up equivalent or better-paid employment elsewhere. The conclusion explains the fact that his career history to date shows frequent changes in employment. The tribunal accepts his evidence that the further up the corporate hierarchy a person climbs within his sort of profession, then the less likely the person is to switch employers. The statistics set out by Mrs Paxton do not support the respondents' claim that he would resign soon'.

'Turning to the respondents' claim that Mr Singh enquires about voluntary redundancy in 2004,' the chairman continues. 'His enquiry is no more than to understand whether voluntary redundancy is available, and is borne out of a frustration at Mr Hobson's attitude at the time. It is never repeated. The enquiry does not support the respondents' claim that he would resign soon'.

'Regarding the matter of the interview Mr Singh attends at another financial institution in the early part of 2005,' the chairman continues. 'Mr Singh accepts he attends the interview. The tribunal places no significance at all on his attendance. To be headhunted seems to be common for employees in his position. The tribunal accepts his testimony that he was targeted for a potential headhunting operation, which, in the event, came to nothing. The attendance of the interview does not support the respondents' submission that he would resign soon'.

'On the grounds the respondents put forward, individually and collectively, the tribunal rejects their submission that Mr Singh would simply resign soon,' the chairman rules. 'He certainly would not leave in order to put himself in a position of disadvantage, like he now finds himself in'.

'Moving on to the matter of whether Mr Singh discharges his legal duty to mitigate his loss,' the chairman says. 'The basic rule of mitigation requires he takes all reasonable steps to mitigate his loss, consequent to the respondents' unlawful conduct. He cannot recover compensation for any loss that he could pre-empt by the taking of reasonable steps, but fails to pre-empt by behaving unreasonably. His duty is limited to acting reasonably. The standard of reasonableness is not high, in view of the fact that he is not the wrongdoer. The onus of proving any alleged failure in his duty is the respondents'. If they fail to show he ought reasonably to take certain mitigating steps for a particular loss, then he is entitled to recover compensation for that loss'.

'In judging the matter of reasonableness,' the chairman continues, 'it is important to consider all of the relevant surrounding circumstances. Turning to the respondents' suggestion that, because he has the prospect of compensation before him, he acts overzealously after the liability hearing in disclosing to prospective employers that he litigated against his former employers. The tribunal is of the overwhelming view that the respondents' suggestion is wholly fallacious. Their suggestion imputes a *dishonest* motive to Mr Singh. The tribunal is completely satisfied he does not volunteer to employers the reasons for his departure from the respondents without the reasons first being elicited from him with direct questions on the subject. The tribunal rejects all suggestions to the effect that he discloses the reasons to employers without the reasons being elicited from him first. The tribunal is satisfied he gives unfairness, race discrimination, and the failure to comply with reinstatement orders, as the reasons only *after* the tribunal formally establishes these facts. The tribunal is satisfied the reason of redundancy he gives prior to the liability hearing is an honest answer of what he believes to be the formal situation at the time. The tribunal rejects the respondents' case on the matter. No question arises whatsoever in the tribunal's mind as to Mr Singh's integrity. The tribunal is completely satisfied he is an entirely honest witness'.

'Failing to find work in his field of expertise, market risk,' the chairman continues, 'Mr Singh contemplates and seeks employment in risk management, risk consultancy, risk sales, financial control, product control, pricing control, valuation control, auditing, and other fields. He gives a very detailed testimony concerning the specific vacancies he applies for, backed up by relevant documentary evidence. The extent of his job search and the extent to which he evidences his attempts to mitigate his loss are *the most thorough, extensive, and well documented* any member of the tribunal can recall having ever seen. The fact that vacancies at his level are so scarce, and the chance of securing junior level roles is so remote, bear out the real fear he expresses. In the light of his continued lack of success in finding another job in the financial sector, the tribunal accepts his decision to pursue an alternative career in teaching as being an entirely reasonable move'.

'The respondents' conduct,' the chairman continues, 'causes Mr Singh the loss of his employment and places him in the position where he cannot, and will not, find another comparable employment. He suffers the loss of his career'.

'Turning now to the matter of the financial damage he suffers consequent to the respondents' unlawful conduct,' the chairman says. 'The damage he sustains comprises of three main categories. They are: *Immediate Loss*; *Future Loss*; and *Pension Loss*'.

'The Immediate Loss,' the chairman continues, 'relates to the time period beginning from the date of his dismissal, and ending on the day the tribunal established liability against the respondents. That is, the eight-month period from April to the 15th of December 2006. Mr Singh is unemployed throughout the whole of this period. His loss for the period is the salary and bonuses he would have earned as though he were employed with the respondents throughout the period. His salary at the time of his dismissal is one hundred thousand pounds per annum'.

Gasps and whispers expressing amazement emanate from the spectators in the public gallery.

'His 2006 annual bonus award,' the chairman continues, 'would be sixty thousand pounds, being the amount the respondents awarded Miss Mykonola, his direct comparator and peer'.

More gasps and whispers expressing astonishment emanate from the public gallery.

'The salary and bonus together,' the chairman continues, 'sum up to a total annual remuneration of one hundred and sixty thousand pounds. On this basis, the tribunal values the Immediate Loss to be one hundred and seven thousand pounds. The loss is subject to accrued simple interest at eight per cent per annum'.

'The Future Loss,' the chairman continues, 'relates to the time period that begins from the day the tribunal established liability against the respondents, and runs into the future to his retirement age. Mr Singh loses his career in the financial sector. He will take up a career in teaching. His Future Loss is effectively the difference between how much he *would* earn in the financial sector and how much he *will* earn in teaching. He expects a salary of twenty-five thousand pounds per annum as a secondary school mathematics teacher. On this basis, and ignoring any future pay rises, the conservative loss he suffers over the future period is one hundred and thirty-five thousand pounds per annum. The actuarial tables assigned to tribunals for the assessment of Future Loss, which take into account the early payments of amounts payable at future dates, inform the tribunal that his loss will run for the equivalent of seventeen years'.

I look across at Neil and Simon and see their jaws drop.

'The tribunal adjusts this figure down,' the chairman continues, 'to sixteen years, to reflect that he may occasionally take some career breaks, as he has done in the past. On this basis, the tribunal determines the Future Loss he suffers to amount to two million, one hundred and sixty thousand pounds'.

Murmurs expressing amazement emanate from the public gallery. With expressions of disbelief on their faces, Neil and Simon shake their heads from side to side.

'The Pension Loss,' the chairman continues, 'relates to the difference between how much he would receive from the respondents' final salary pension scheme, and how much he will receive from a final salary scheme available in teaching. His final salary at the bank would be much higher than it will be in teaching. The actuarial tables and calculation formulae assigned to tribunals for assessing Pension Loss determine the loss he suffers to amount to four hundred and fifty thousand pounds'.

More mutterings expressing astonishment emanate from the public gallery.

'On the matter of distress and *Injury to Feelings*,' the chairman continues. 'The respondents cause Mr Singh considerable unnecessary distress and hurt by their conduct and manners. They could have assuaged the injuries by making a prompt apology, or an admission of wrongdoing, at the end of the liability hearing, even though they denied any wrongdoing to begin with, and then, by adopting a reasonable approach in the matter of remedy. Instead, they choose not to acknowledge they racially discriminated against him. The injuries to feelings are perpetuated by their failure to accept they racially discriminated against him, and by their stance that they did nothing wrong whatsoever. In the circumstances, the tribunal considers right to make an Injury to Feelings award amounting to fifteen thousand pounds, out of the permitted twenty-five thousand pounds maximum'.

'Moving on now to the penalties incurred in the circumstances,' the chairman says.

'For their failure to comply with the reinstatement orders,' the chairman continues, 'the respondents are liable to the payment of an *Additional Award*. The size of the award is dependent on the length of the time period spanning from the date of Mr Singh's dismissal to the day the tribunal established the respondents' compliance failure. In the circumstances, the Additional Award amounts to eleven thousand pounds'.

'On the matter of the respondents' failures to follow the statutory redundancy procedures,' the chairman continues. 'The respondents' failure is substantial. By their failure, they deny Mr Singh the protection the procedures intend to afford employees. The bank is a large organisation with a professional Human Resources department that should not make the mistakes it does. It is familiar with the procedures. It should comply with them. The department fails to serve any party anywhere near as well as it ought to'.

I look across at Veronica and see her cringe.

'An *Uplift Penalty* of thirty-five per cent,' the chairman continues, 'would be entirely correct in the circumstances, being towards the top end of the permitted ten per cent to fifty per cent range. The uplift percentage applies to the whole of the loss suffered, except to the Additional Award amount'.

That multiplies out to a penalty of *one million pounds*! I look across at Veronica again. Her jaw drops, her face turns pale.

'The tribunal is mindful,' the chairman continues, 'that the total loss suffered is very high in this case, and a thirty-five per cent uplift will result in a huge penalty in monetary terms. In the interest of justice, the uplift percentage ought not to be set at this level. The large size of the total loss suffered is an exceptional factor entitling the tribunal to make an uplift penalty that is *below* even the ten per cent minimum level, or even to make *no* penalty at all'.

An expression of heartfelt relief diffuses over Veronica's face; the colour that had deserted it begins to return.

'The purpose of the uplift penalty,' the chairman continues, 'is to penalise the respondents for their failures to comply with the statutory redundancy procedures. Their failures are substantial. Not to make any uplift penalty whatsoever would be unsatisfactory, given their substantial failures. In the circumstances, the tribunal considers appropriate to set an uplift of two per cent'.

That multiplies out to a *fifty thousand pounds* penalty. It is not insignificant. Veronica's face falls.

'Taking into account a two per cent uplift,' the chairman continues, 'the tribunal establishes the total financial loss Mr Singh suffers, consequent to the respondents' unlawful conduct, amounts to two million, eight hundred and three thousand, seven hundred and eleven pounds'.

Mumblings expressing amazement emanate from the public gallery. I am grateful the tribunal recognises the proper extent of the damage the respondents cause me. But, the ruling does not relieve my nerves. Thus far, the tribunal has merely established the magnitude of my loss. How much of it will it decide to award me as compensation, if any at all? I can only await the answer with bated breath.

'The tribunal must now consider how much of the established loss may be rightly awarded under the legal remedy of compensation,' the chairman says. 'The respondents submit that Mr Singh is to blame for his dismissal, and that his loss must be diminished to zero to reflect this. They submit he brings the dismissal upon himself by hostile, ill-judged, perverse, foolish, bloody-minded conduct towards Mr Hobson. The tribunal recognises there is a conflict of personalities between the two of them. It is a conflict they both are able to cope with in the sense that they maintain a good professional working relationship. The tribunal finds Mr Singh does not conduct himself in any way the respondents claim that he does. He does not contribute to his dismissal, whatsoever, by any culpable conduct. No deduction to his loss can be rightly made in this respect'.

The ruling pleases me, but still my nerves are not reduced; one potentially award-quashing test is passed safely, but another still remains to be faced.

'Regarding his duty to mitigate his loss,' the chairman

continues, 'the tribunal finds the respondents do not demonstrate in any way whatsoever that he fails. No deduction to the loss can be rightly made in this respect either'.

Phew! The ruling relieves my nerves completely. I am grateful the tribunal sees fit to order the respondents to compensate me in full for the damage they cause me. My counsel twists around to face me. With a face lit up by heartfelt joy, she gives me a double thumbs-up gesture. I acknowledge her with a subtle nod only, maintaining a poker face and a still exterior. I dare not show any feelings until after the judgement is delivered completely, for fear of jinxing it.

Neil, Simon, and Veronica, with grave worry apparent in their faces, sit stunned.

'Under the circumstances,' the chairman continues, 'the respondents must indemnify Mr Singh in *full* for the entire loss he sustains. The tribunal makes a Compensation Award against the respondents for two million, eight hundred and three thousand, seven hundred and eleven pounds. The tribunal's decision is unanimous'.

My counsel, facing forwards towards the judges, extends her right arm backwards towards me, passing me a note, like a child in a classroom. I reach forwards and take it. It reads: *a record-breaking compensation, by a mile! Previous record £1.4M. Yours is double. Congrats!* The thought delights me that she can add an epic success of a record-breaking compensation award to her list of professional achievement.

Sweet is the other side of the coin; the respondents' belligerent pitch for a zero compensation award backfiring to end as a record-breaking, history making, multi-million pound, epic failure. Priceless is that they have only themselves to blame. To think, they refused the certainties of reinstatement, brought compensation back into play, to then endeavour to diminish it to nothing, only to fail on a grand scale.

I am grateful for fortunate personal circumstances that permitted me to reach this far. I feel relief, but no sense of jubilation, though, for this might only be the end of a stage, not necessarily completion of the whole process. I fear the respondents will not allow the matter to rest here.

Addressing the respondents' counsel, the chairman asks, 'do you wish to make any statement on behalf of the respondents?'

She turns around and confers in private whispers with Neil, Simon, and Veronica.

I dread what they are discussing, unless she is advising them of the many benefits of reinstatement, and recommending serious reconsideration and application of the remedy at this juncture. Despite demonstrating considerable goodwill towards them, despite giving them ample opportunity to avoid litigation, and then despite presenting them with the chance to end this matter amicably and avoid financial compensation altogether, they remain hard and belligerent towards me. The record-breaking magnitude of the compensation award against them will probably rile them even more. They have deep pockets. They can afford to perpetuate costly litigation for as long as it takes to get their way, whether by legal decisions in their favour, or by suppressing me into submission, either by frustration, or by crushing me under severe financial hardship where, because I must bear my own costs in seeking justice, I am forced to stop pursuing them for running out of money. They will exploit fully every single opportunity available to them to be troublesome, in the knowledge that they will manage comfortably, while I struggle. For them, this is like a game; for me, there are real life consequences.

The rational risk controller in me seeks solace in thinking there is a good chance, though, in the face of a record-breaking two point eight million pounds compensation award, which the newspapers are bound to pick up on and splatter across their front pages, that they are revisiting reinstatement seriously as a cheap and certain course for limiting financial and reputational damage.

'Sir,' she answers upon finishing conferring, 'the respondents are confident of being able to present strong cases to appeal the matters of liability and remedy'.

Printed in Great Britain
by Amazon